THAT'S THE SPIRIT

RENEE JOINER

Oshun
PUBLICATIONS
oshunpublications.com

RENEE JOINER

that's the
spirit

Oshun
Publications

Book design by Bella Hudson

www.belladesignstudios.com

Published by Oshun Publications

www.oshunpublications.com

Did you know you can take every story with you?

I know it's tough these days to simply find the time to relax and curl up with a good book. This is why I'm delighted to share that I have books available in audio book format.

Best of all, you can get the audio book version of any book by me for free as part of a 30-day Audible trial.

Members get free audio books every month and exclusive discounts. It's an excellent way to explore and determine if audio book learning works for you.

If you're not satisfied, you can cancel anytime within the trial period. You won't be charged, and you can even keep your audio book.

To choose a free audio book, click on your favorite title's cover to be taken to Audible's website for details.

Remember, there's no obligation to buy.

reneejoinerauthor.com/audiobooks

JOIN MY NEWSLETTER
GET UPDATES, FREEBIES & GIVEAWAYS
RENEEJOINERAUTHOR.COM/NEWSLETTER

Singles by Renee

Singles
Tempest
Half Demon
Wanted Undead or Alive
My Soul to Reap
Gravetide
Vance and Vance
Cold Read
Witch's Justice

ONE

The Séance

THE UNSEASONABLE RAIN POUNDED AGAINST THE WINDOWS of the occult shop. The summer humidity and poor weather meant few customers would bother to venture out. Rylee leaned against the countertop of the empty shop as her day dragged on. She effectively lived at her uncle's shop these days. At the age of twenty, she spent most of her days restocking crystals and informing occult enthusiasts and beginners about herbs' nuances.

She was a short thing, something her handful of friends and remaining family loved to remind her of. At only five-foot-two, she didn't have much in the way of physical presence. She kept her brown hair long, probably in an attempt to make up for her lack of height.

Rylee didn't have many friends. Otherwise, she would be dodging the weather with them at a theater or college party. She also didn't have much family; her parents died in a car accident nearly five years ago. After their deaths, she moved in with her uncle and helped with the shop. Even now that she had her own place, he still helped her out now and then.

Her uncle liked to brag about her abilities. She was a powerful medium that held the best séances in town. Or so the sign said. Rylee didn't love the advertising, but she couldn't deny that she had a strong connection with the spirit world. She could talk to them without trying; they would reach out to her, and she could help them move on if needed. She was also a moderately gifted empath and able to feel others' emotions, although that was easier with ghosts.

A lot of people had powers. It was so common that her own abilities seemed mundane compared to some of the others around her. Some people, like her, could talk to the dead. Some were more than mediums; they were Reapers and could control the dead. Others had powers that didn't relate to the dead at all.

And then there were the ones, like her uncle, without any powers. Sometimes she thought he was jealous, and that's why he kept her chained to the family shop.

The phone rang, stealing Rylee away from her thoughts. "A Daily Dose of Crystal, Rylee speaking, how can we fill your obscure needs?" Rylee had mastered her mystical customer service voice.

The customer, on the other end, mumbled something about crystals and their current stock. Rylee answered before giving them a polite but brief goodbye.

Stretching her legs, Rylee wandered to the incense section, making sure they were well stocked and neat. She had to do something to pass the time. Her uncle insisted on keeping the store open until 9 p.m., regardless of how many customers came in. He didn't care since he was not the one stuck in the store alone.

She wasn't really alone. The spirits around the shop touched at the edges of her mind. Most were pleasant.

Others were not. This was unusual. Even if she could sense them now and then, they were rarely able to reach out as they were.

The day finally came to a close. Rylee locked up for the night before heading home. The rain had stopped, but a strange chill had settled in around her. She walked the three short blocks to her apartment. She lived nearby to help her uncle as needed. She may not always enjoy it, but the shop was hers as much as his and she did appreciate the legacy.

"Rylee!"

The voice was clear, ringing whispered and distant all at once. Rylee looked around but couldn't find anyone nearby. She was alone on the doorstep of her apartment. There were spirits around but none so present they could talk to her like that. She felt a slight chill and hurried inside, locking the door behind her.

Rylee was exhausted and found herself on autopilot as she got ready for bed. Curling up, she drifted off to sleep. Her dreams were filled with spirits and violence. She saw bodies dripping with blood and mysterious forms stalking unaware victims. She woke many times in a cold sweat and fearful.

Even after a fitful night's sleep, Rylee still had to help her uncle at the store. A Daily Dose of Crystal had been in their family for generations; it was their legacy. She was not about to be the reason it closed.

Plus, she thought with some pride, not many mediums can help souls like I can.

She got dressed and grabbed her bag. The shop would be busier today; Saturdays always went by much faster, and the weather improved.

As Rylee locked her apartment, she felt a strange sensation run up her spine. She figured a window was open somewhere and shrugged it off. Still, when she got outside, she noticed that the chill in the air from the night before had not lifted, and it gave her an uneasy feeling. Something strange was going on around this town. She tried to push those thoughts out of her mind as she arrived at her family shop and got ready to open up.

Even though her uncle was supposed to be there before her, he was always late. Sometimes, he wouldn't show up until two hours after she opened, leaving her and Ava, the part-time clerk, to fend for themselves. Today was no different. Rylee went through her typical routine of opening the till and saying a prayer over the crystals before Ava came in to help her restock.

Ava was younger than Rylee, although she didn't look it with her height. Ava had pale skin and straight blond hair to the middle of her back. She had a good work ethic that was hard to find in teenagers these days. It helped that she looked up to Rylee for reasons that even Rylee couldn't fathom. The clock struck nine, and Ava unlocked the doors. They had a few regulars first thing in the morning that needed to stock up on various ingredients for their potions and remedies or replenish their incenses.

Ava and Rylee were in a good flow when Rylee saw her Uncle Tarsizio. His rather unkempt appearance always stood out; his greying hair was never combed, and his shirt seemed comically large on his slender frame. Rylee nodded to him as he entered before returning her attention to the customers and their crystal-related questions.

"You might want onyx or quartz. They're good all-around crystals," she explained as the customer listened intently.

She explained what the dark blue crystal, known as azurite, did when she heard her name called again in the same distant ringing tone. This time she was sure; spirits were calling to her. She brushed it off since azurite was known to increase psychic abilities. That must be the only reason the spirits had been so loud in her head. She showed the customers a few more crystals, and each one chose a few to take home with them.

"Did you hear about that poor boy a couple nights ago?" a customer said in a hushed tone to her companion.

"What? No? What happened?" the companion asked, lowering her voice to match.

Rylee froze from the other side of the shelves. She felt their eagerness for gossip and their fear even through the shelves. She pretended to stock the shelves with more tarot decks. That was the good thing about working in a store like this; she was invisible.

"Oh, he was barely in his twenties. Found with his throat slit and dumped in an alley. Had a note on him, but the police refused to say what was in it. As they always do. It was probably meant for them, the corrupt pigs."

"Another gang death, then?"

"Are there any other types lately? That's the ninth one this week!"

Rylee didn't need to hear the rest of it. She already knew that the local gangs increased their violence. That was evident by the influx of spirits. Still, hearing about such a young death was sad, even if it was all too common.

Rival gangs liked to bring Powered People into their ranks. Lots of them died in fights over territory or even fights over other Powered individuals. Others would sometimes drag children in. Rylee counted herself lucky that her powers weren't on their radar. Being a medium was cool, but it didn't make her valuable to the city's violent-prone parts.

Rylee moved on with her day. The after-lunch rush was

when everyone seemed to have a million questions for her. She was being pulled in every direction, and her head was starting to hurt. She felt the spirits calling to her even louder even though she was nowhere near the crystals. She felt a pounding pressure in her head. She could tell something was going on, and she needed to escape the noise of the shop floor to figure out what it was. The shop quieted down a bit, and it seemed like her Uncle Tarsizio and Ava had it under control for now, and Ava would be heading home soon. Rylee slipped into the back room and then behind the secret door that she didn't think even her uncle knew was there.

Once in the dimly lit back room, Rylee pulled her own crystals from her bag and lit some frankincense incense. She arranged a few candles in a circle around her and burned them in order. She centered herself in the ring of fire as the fragrance filled the room. Focusing her energy, she called out to the spirits of the world beyond her own.

"Welcome, spirits," she said. The candles on the floor flickered. "You seem eager to speak to me today."

She felt the spirits arriving and answering her call. There were more than she expected. The incense smoke filled her nose and grounded her against their clamoring voices. They were able to manifest with her link. Vague shadows and ghostly forms appeared at the edge of the candlelight.

"What's causing this unusual chill in town? And why are there so many of you?" she asked.

She was bombarded with dozens of voices at once, each offering different answers, and some shouting names she didn't recognize. Others tried to get her attention by touching her, but the incense and crystals kept them from doing so.

Most mediums that Rylee knew could communicate with spirits. Still, she didn't know anyone else who could help them cross over to the other side. That was something only Rylee seemed to have. It made her more popular with the local spirits; they seemed to know and were drawn to her as a result. It didn't help that she could also feel what they were feeling. Spirits were often simple and held onto the last memory or emotion they felt—the room filled with a thick, mournful fear that pressed into Rylee's heart and throat.

Many of the spirits around her were stuck between her reality and the beyond. They needed help crossing over, as she had done before. Swallowing that fear, Rylee promised that she would help them in any way she could.

As they were all trying to talk to her at once, she noticed that most of these spirits looked familiar. With some horror, she recognized them from her nightmares. Upon closer inspection, they also matched descriptions of local gang members.

What's going on? Rylee wondered, trying to communicate with all of the spirits around her. This was not normal.

"Tell me, spirits, why are you here?" Rylee asked. A handful of spirits wasn't unusual. This was dozens.

One of the spirits responded, "We want to know who is killing us!"

"Show us your best work, girl," another said, pushing his way to the front. "I want to see you perform!"

Rylee was slightly taken aback. She was no detective. She didn't know how to find out who was killing them. "I'll do my best. What do you remember?"

"Shouldn't you know that little girl?" the spirit asked back spitefully.

Okay then, they are not going to make this easy, Rylee thought.

She centered herself and began to get visions of what happened in the past 72 hours. Some of these spirits had been stabbed, choked, or shot; it was like someone had a hit list and was simply checking them off of it. It wasn't just one person. It seemed that there was a whole group of people working off of this one list, working for someone who controlled everything.

Those who didn't hold on to their deaths' exact image were filled with rage and hate. Impressions of deep loathing filled her, making her muscles tense. She clenched her jaw to keep their feelings from overriding her own.

"I see that there is one person who wanted all of you dead, I cannot quite figure out who he is, but he is powerful," Rylee said as her visions came to a close. She lit some more incense and breathed the scent in deeply. "You are all from different gangs and organizations; who could be trying to shut you all down?"

"B.G.," one of the ghosts in the back said quietly.

"What was that?" Rylee asked, tuning in to this young man.

"Some big name on the street. New guy. Has all the gangs on edge now," the young man explained. "We started calling him Mr. Bad Guy since we don't know his real name. Everyone calls him Mr. B.G. or B.G. for short now.

Rylee closed her eyes. She could see a figure shrouded in darkness. That could have been him. "I see someone but am not sure if it's the man you are describing."

That angered the spirits around her. Gang members weren't known for their patience and understanding natures. They pushed at the edge of the light, and the flames on the candles flickered with their efforts.

That's enough, Rylee decided, blowing out the candles, severing the connection. The spirits started to dissipate, but one more spirit came through before she could close her link to the spirit realm.

"Rylee!" he said urgently.

His voice was familiar. Was this the one she heard before? "How do you know my name?" Rylee was a little concerned at his intensity.

"I have a message for you," he replied. "My name is Ewan. Make everyone leave! I don't want them to hear!"

Rylee felt something was different about this spirit. She knew that she had a deep connection with the spirit world, even more so than many other mediums she knew. Still, even that didn't come close to the level of connection she felt with this spirit.

"You said your name was Ewan?" Rylee asked cautiously.

"Yeah, nice to meet you, Miss Rylee," he responded. There was still a sense of urgency in his voice, but it had softened quite a bit. Ewan was at least six feet tall. He had messy hair, but Rylee couldn't tell what color it was in his spectral form. Ewan was muscular but not obnoxiously huge. Rylee could tell that he had only been dead for a few days. His spirit was still young.

Was this the guy those ladies were talking about? He looks to be about the right age. She carefully examined the spectral being in front of her while still keeping a gentle disposition. She saw where his throat had been slit. This had to be him.

"Nice to meet you too, Ewan," Rylee said with a smile. "What is this message you have for me? What could be so urgent?"

The rest of the spirits were fading away as Rylee released her connection with them. A few were more stubborn and wanted answers, but Rylee was stronger than they were and got them to move along back to the spirit world. When only a couple of spirits remained with a loose grasp on the connection, Rylee looked back to Ewan. "Please tell me the message," she said.

"Someone wants you dead, Miss Rylee! They wanted your parents dead, and now they want you dead," Ewan explained. His voice was quiet, barely above a whisper.

Rylee's heart sank. It was a lot to take in at once. Someone had been out for her parent's lives, and now hers?

"Someone wants me dead?" Rylee repeated. "But, why? I don't understand."

"I can tell you more once these bozos leave, but you have to believe me, Rylee," Ewan pleaded with her.

Rylee didn't need her powers to feel the desperation in the spirit's voice. Those only added to it. He was in anguish as if his last feelings were urgent and panicked, but also somehow determined. Yet, she wasn't sure if they were his last living emotions. He was so full of them now, but there was a lack of anything older.

Rylee paused, "I—I do believe you. I believe you more than I have ever believed anyone before." Rylee buried her face in her hands; she did not have the energy to process everything Ewan had just told her. She also needed to know why she had such a strong connection with him.

Why do I believe this man? What is it about him? She thought, could this be what I think it is? It seemed impossible.

"Rylee, I am so glad that you believe me; I want to keep you safe," Ewan said meekly.

"Thanks for warning me, Ewan," Rylee sighed.

That seemed to seal the deal; the only reason a spirit would want to keep a specific medium safe was if that medium was their soul mate. If that spirit couldn't be with them in life, they would protect them in death. She sat with this thought and ultimately released the last of the spirits that lingered.

I have a soul mate, she thought. And he's dead.

TWO

Danger Arises

"WE ARE ALONE NOW, EWAN; PLEASE TELL ME WHAT'S going on," Rylee pleaded with him.

"All I know right now is that you're in danger. I don't have many memories from before I died. It's like someone took control of me. I feel lost, Rylee," Ewan explained. The pain on his face was evident.

Rylee felt the weight of that feeling in his soul. There was so much needed to be figured out before he could move on and fully transition to the Beyond. Other than his emotions, that was all she felt, which made it even odder. Usually, she could feel where a soul was heading after death and whether they had been good or bad people when they were alive. She felt none of that with Ewan. All she felt was emptiness. She knew that it was no accident that he found her on this day; he needed to be with her.

"Ewan, there has to be something you remember," Rylee said softly.

"No!" Ewan shouted. "I need you to help me get my memories back! I know you can do it."

Rylee was surprised. "What do you mean you know I can help you?"

"I am drawn to you, Rylee. My soul knows that you're important. But I also know that you are in great danger. Somehow these things are related, but until I get my memories back, I can't explain any more than that." Ewan was getting flustered. The spirit was pacing around the room.

"Okay, okay, I understand. I will do everything I can to help you get your memories back," Rylee conceded. "We will need a place to start, but I will help you in any way I can."

"Rylee, that means so much to me!" Ewan did a flip in midair. Glee radiated off his spectral form. "Do you have any idea where we can begin? I have never been dead before."

"Oh, so now we're making jokes?" Rylee snapped.

Ewan blushed as much as a spirit could.

"I'm not really sure," Rylee continued. "I know I have a stronger connection to the dead than other mediums, so I might be able to channel that to find a starting point."

Rylee moved the table to the side and found new candles to light. She wanted to start a new séance with just Ewan so she could focus on his energy and his spirit. She lit more frankincense, as well as some lemongrass for memory and patchouli to help her deepen her connection with the spirit world. She wanted to stop anything from blocking her as she looked into Ewan's past. She grounded herself on one of her favorite rugs, closed her eyes, and worked to travel into the spirit world to find what was missing from Ewan's soul and memory.

Just as she was starting to make a connection, she was jolted out of her trance by Ewan. "Rylee! Miss Rylee!"

Rylee was still coming back to the physical world.

Dazed and disoriented, she turned to the ghost and snapped, "Ewan! I am trying to help you!"

"You don't understand! I just saw something! We need to get out of here! NOW!" Ewan was talking faster.

Rylee got up. She grabbed her coat and her bag; something about Ewan's urgency spoke to her. "Ewan, what did you see?" she asked.

"Someone is coming! I see it!" he told her. He really wanted to get her out of there. "No, it isn't just one, multiple people are coming, and they want to hurt you badly!"

Rylee didn't need any more information; Ewan clearly cared about her. She grabbed a few essential items and crystals and sprinted into the center of the closing store. "Uncle Tars, please, someone is coming, I can't explain it, but you need to come with me!"

"Little Rylee-bear, I will be fine," Uncle Tarsizio told her. "I am just locking up. I will close the till and leave soon. Nobody is coming after either of us."

Rylee wanted to scream in his face. He needed her to keep this shop running, but he still treated her like a little kid sometimes. He knew she had connections to the spirit world and used that to his advantage whenever he could, but he didn't want to believe her now.

"Well, I am getting out of here. It isn't safe," Rylee said. "Please, Uncle Tars, please come with me!"

Once again, Tarsizio refused. Resigned, Rylee crept towards the back exit.

Rylee had just snuck out the back door when she heard a bang, a clatter of metal on the ground, and the shop's front door swings open. She snuck around, keeping as quiet as she could, and saw three prominent figures making their way into the shop. She needed to get out of there.

She ran down the alley, using all of her senses to make

sure nobody could spot her. She was vaguely aware of Ewan following beside her, but her focus was on escaping. She didn't know who was after her, so she couldn't know where they had eyes looking out for her. It could have been any gang. She never interacted with any of them, and her powers weren't particularly useful to her. Why would they want her?

Once she was a safe distance away from the shop, and it was evident that nobody had followed her, she sank to the ground to rest for a moment.

Rylee was eternally grateful to Ewan's vision and his insistence. She didn't want to think what would have happened if those men had found her mid-trance and absolutely helpless. She cringed at the thought. She needed to be more careful; she couldn't reach out to the ghostly realm without someone watching her back until this was all sorted out. That would make things a little more compli-cated since Ewan was a spirit; the most he could do is get her attention, not actively defend her.

"Are you okay, Rylee?" Ewan asked cautiously, not wanting to spook her.

Rylee looked at him, feeling appreciation and affection that wasn't there before at the sight of him. "I think I am," she said. "Thank you so much, Ewan. If you hadn't warned me, that could have gone very badly. There's a reason you are in my life; we need to figure out what that is."

"All I care about is that you are safe, Miss Rylee," Ewan said, "I need to know more about my past, and I think the two are related. I just don't understand why."

"Let me text my uncle; I need to know that he is okay. I hate that I left him behind," Rylee fretted, searching for her phone in her bag.

Rylee: Hey Uncle Tars, I'm safe. I hope you are too.

Tars: My Rylee-bear, I am happy to hear you are safe. Don't worry about me. I know how to handle myself. I am okay.

Rylee: I'm so happy to hear that! I hated that I left you behind. Please stay safe!

Tars: Rylee, calm your mind. I will be okay, I promise.

Rylee: I love you, Uncle Tars.

Tars: I love you too, my Rylee-bear.

"Well, at least I know he is safe," Rylee sighed, "for now, that is."

"At least one of us is," Ewan said.

Rylee looked at him; her heart felt like it was going to fly into a million pieces. Could she actually be falling in love with this spirit? Of course, if they really were soul mates, it made sense, all that existed of him was his soul, and she had a deep connection to it because she was a medium. Love was inevitable. She wasn't quite ready to share that little piece of information with him yet; she needed more time. Part of her wondered if he felt it too. Would he, as a spirit?

"I guess we're a team now," Rylee said. She was trying to think of what to do next while they were protected from all lines of sight in the dark alley.

In desperation, she began to pray, seeking help from the gods and spirits around her. There was no altar, no natural offerings of acorns or fallen leaves, just her words. She needed to know that she and Ewan were not alone in this. It felt daunting. She was barely an adult; she lost her parents; she loved her uncle, but he was not the most upstanding citizen. She had nobody in this world that she could trust. She was not ready to die, and she was so afraid of what was coming for her, none of this seemed fair.

She moved her quartz crystal from her bag to her bra; she had sewn in a special pocket into all of her bras for when she needed extra protection. It was a very personal touch that she felt she needed. Ewan didn't look the slightest bit phased as she finished her prayer and settled it into the pocket. Still, his eyes did linger on her breasts a moment more extended than would have been considered proper if he were alive.

"I am not ready to die, Ewan. We have to fight them." Rylee felt overwhelmed and exhausted. How could things have changed so much in just a few hours? She thought her parents died in an accident. She believed she only had typical connections to spirits, just like the other mediums she knew. She would never have imagined that someone wanted her dead.

Ewan tried to calm her down. The spirit moved closer. "Rylee, it's okay. We will figure it out. You are stronger than you know; you have a deeper connection to the spirit world than any other medium I have felt. I was drawn to you for a reason."

"Ewan, my entire life has just been turned upside down!" Rylee shouted before she remembered that she didn't want anyone to find her. "Sorry, you are the only one I have right now. I am just so…" she stopped mid-sentence; what word would describe how she felt, scared, angry, and alone? None of those words felt strong enough to her.

She sat in silence for a while before deciding that now was as good a time as any to get moving and start figuring out what would trigger Ewan's memory.

"My apartment is just a few blocks away from the shop. I need to gather a few things before we can get started. This might be dangerous, but there are things that my parents left for me that might help," Rylee said more for her own benefit than Ewan's.

THREE

Finding Memories

THEY SNUCK BACK THROUGH THE ALLEY TO GET TO Rylee's building. Just as she was about to make a run to get to the front door, her phone buzzed.

"What does Uncle Tarsizio want? I told him I am safe." She was visibly annoyed, she was too close to danger for any distractions, but she opened the message anyway.

Tars: Rylee-bear, the danger has passed, please come back to the shop.

Rylee: Why would I come back? Just because nobody is there now doesn't mean they won't return.

Tars: We have a lot of clean-up to do from the break-in. I still plan to open tomorrow. You have to come.

Rylee: It isn't safe, Uncle Tars! Did you even call the police? Did you file a report?

Tars: Of course, it is safe. The police have been made aware. Just sleep on it. Tomorrow is a new day.

"Are you okay?" Ewan asked as she put her phone back in her pocket.

"Something weird is going on with my uncle, but I don't know what. He wanted me back at the store! Can you believe it?" Rylee was dumbfounded. "Let's get my stuff and get out of here."

She made sure the coast was clear, and she quickly snuck into the building, managing to avoid any nosey neighbors. She was cautious as she opened her apartment door. Anyone could jump out and overtake her without much of a fight, given her height. Luckily, nobody was there, and she was able to grab some of her spell books, a few crystals from her altar, and plenty of incense.

While she was barely a young adult when her parents died, she had picked up a lot of knowledge about building temporary altars and performing her craft on the go. At least her parents left her with that. They were mediums themselves, but they had only just started to teach her about it when they died. She didn't even have her powers until after the accident.

She grabbed a change of clothes and packed everything away in her backpack. She needed to be able to move quickly, so she had to be a little picky about which books she could bring. She wanted to bring them all but settled on a small handful of general books instead of specific topics.

She also didn't want it to be apparent that she had been there and that she was on the run. She was sure that the men that were after her would go to her apartment at some point if they hadn't been through it already. If all her books and clothes were gone, it would be obvious to anyone that she had been through here already. She flitted around her apartment and threw her brown curly hair into a loose ponytail that bounced behind her as she tried to think of everything she could need.

"Okay, Ewan, I think I have everything. Let's get out of here before we have any unwanted company," Rylee said with a shaky voice.

"I couldn't agree more," Ewan said. "It's going to be okay, Rylee. I believe in you. I was drawn to you for a reason."

His gaze lingered on her for a moment. Rylee wasn't sure what she saw in his eyes before they darted away. Hope, maybe? Or was it affection? Now's not really the time to act like a schoolgirl, she thought. Still, they were soul mates that much she knew.

Rylee locked the door behind her as she stealthily left the building to make it back to the alleyway. She hadn't seen Ewan around her neighborhood, so he must live outside of her tight-knit part of town.

Well, lived, she thought. He was dead, after all.

Using the alleyways, she made her way out of the area before stopping to regroup. She needed a plan before she was willing to go out onto the streets.

"Ewan, we need something to start with. Can you see anything that is remotely familiar?" Rylee pressed gently.

"I am trying," Ewan screwed up his face trying to force his memory to work, "there is a building I can see."

Rylee gave a small, whispered cheer. "Yes! That's what I am talking about! Tell me about it, Ewan." Rylee continued to walk down the unfamiliar alleyways as Ewan tried to focus. She had no idea where she was, and she hoped that the guys after her would never think to look for her here.

"The building is out of place on the street. It has a red brick facade, and every other one has brown," Ewan was thinking out loud, "I would, umm…"

"Ewan, you are doing great. Keep it up!" Rylee encouraged him. She felt his energy pulling at her; she wanted to hug him so badly. She was sure they were going to find the building soon.

"Oh! Yes! I would get ice cream from the little store on

the corner on my way home," Ewan remembered. "I would get a chocolate cone and finish it just as I was unlocking my apartment door."

This information was beneficial; Rylee was starting to understand how his block looked. If he had enough time to eat an ice cream cone between leaving the ice cream shop and opening his door, it had to be a long block. However, it couldn't be too long if he walked the whole way; he lived on a major road. She pulled her phone back out and ignored the latest text from her uncle; she had more important things to worry about now. She looked up ice cream shops in their town and started showing them to Ewan. She hoped that he would recognize one of them as the one near his home.

She went through six different places, and none of them jogged his memory; she was nervous that this would be pointless. As she moved to the seventh one, Ewan paused a moment, something sparkling in his eyes.

"This is it! This is my corner!" Ewan closed his eyes as if remembering the taste of the homemade chocolate ice cream. They were just two blocks from the address; Rylee picked up her pace and arrived at the ice cream store in no time.

Rylee hadn't even noticed that the sun was starting to come up. They had been on the run all night. They were starting to get somewhere, and the adrenaline was pumping through her veins. Once she determined that most of the block was quiet, she straightened her jacket, took her hair out of its ponytail, shook it out, and relaxed her shoulders. She needed to look natural walking down the street, or someone would notice. Despite the early hour, there were still a few people that seemed to be up for whatever reason dragged people out of bed at dawn on a Sunday morning.

She and Ewan talked as she walked down the block. Ewan told her about how he lived in this area for a long time; he was starting to remember a few things as different sights triggered memories. He remembered playing hand-ball with his friends when he was young on a street similar to this one. But something bothered him. Those memories seemed so long ago; for some reason, he stopped playing with them after just a couple of years.

Rylee's heart broke for him, she could see that he desperately wanted to remember, but something was blocking him. Before she could ask more questions about his childhood, he stopped in front of a big red building, just like he had described.

"This is it, Rylee, this is where I lived," he said mournfully.

"Alright, are you ready to start getting to the bottom of this?" Rylee asked as she took an intense breath.

"I don't really have a choice; we can't stay on the street forever," Ewan reminded her. "The guys who are after you could have eyes anywhere. You need cover, and I need answers."

Rylee couldn't agree more. One of his neighbors was just leaving. She confidently walked up to the front door, catching the door before it locked. She decided the easiest way to find his apartment was to look at the mailboxes. Since Ewan just died, his name should still be on the box. That was when she realized that she had no idea what Ewan's last name was.

"Umm, Ewan," she started, "all of these mailboxes only have first initials and last names. Do you remember your last name?"

Ewan paused to think. He had to have a last name, right? "I think it started with a P," he determined. While this wasn't a ton of information to go off of, it was better than nothing; they began scouring the mailboxes for the initials' E.P.'

"I found it!" Rylee called him over, "E. Peters, apartment 412, let's go!"

She bounded for the stairs and took them two at a time. Ewan followed behind closely. She came to a halt on the fourth floor and caught her breath; she needed to get into the apartment, but the door was still locked. She wondered if anyone even knew that Ewan was dead or if anybody even cared.

"Ewan," she said carefully, "we need to get into your apartment, but I don't know how to pick locks."

Ewan looked at her with sympathy. The spirit through the hall, as if searching for something or distressed. He approached her almost as if to hug her before returning to his pacing. "Why do I have to be a ghost?!" he exclaimed, startling her.

The door on the opposite side of the hall opened. A tall, elderly man appeared. He had a kind, but weathered face and his grey hair was neatly brushed.

"That's Mr. Kildare. He's fantastic," Ewan said.

"Hello, young lady, how are you today?" Mr. Kildare asked. "I don't believe I've seen you before."

"Oh, hello, I am alright. I'm a friend of Ewan's. He told me all about you, Mr. Kildare," Rylee responded, trying to play it cool. "It's nice to finally meet you! How are you this morning?"

"Mr. Kildare keeps a spare key for me in case I lock myself out," Ewan whispered. He didn't need to; he could have said it or even shouted it. It wasn't like Mr. Kildare could hear him in his current state.

"Well, thank you," Mr. Kildare smiled. "Young Ewan always has such nice friends."

"I was actually wondering if you still had Ewan's spare

key. He asked me to grab a few things from his apartment but forgot to give me his keys," Rylee came up with a lie on the spot and hoped it was believable.

"Ah yes, Ewan is a sweet young boy. I keep his key right by my door," Mr. Kildare grabbed the fluffy rabbit's foot keychain that held Ewan's spare key and gently tossed it to Rylee. "He always keeps the strangest hours. I always wonder what he's up to."

"Oh, thank you, Sir! I am so grateful." Rylee hoped that she wasn't laying it on too thick. "I will get this back to you later today."

"No rush, sweetie," Mr. Kildare told her, "I will be around if you need anything. Tell Ewan I have the ingredients for his favorite lunch if he wants to stop by sometime soon."

Rylee smiled and nodded before disappearing into Ewan's apartment and closing the door behind her. She sunk onto Ewan's couch and tried to take in everything that happened to her in the last 24 hours.

She just wanted to wake up and realize this is all a bizarre dream and see her parents in the kitchen making breakfast. Maybe these last five years never happened. She laughed to herself; she was too old to believe that this was her reality, and she just needed to face the facts. If she wanted to survive, she needed to get to work figuring out this whole crazy mess.

FOUR

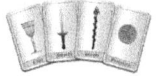

Windows to the Past

RYLEE AND EWAN STARTED SEARCHING THE APARTMENT immediately. Ewan couldn't do much in his state; he couldn't open drawers, pick up papers, or so much as shimmy a candle flame.

"Gah! This is so infuriating!" Ewan snapped.

Rylee looked at him with some pity and, despite her best attempts to fight it, yawned. "I'm sorry, Ewan, but if I am going to be of any use to you, I desperately need to sleep," Rylee said. "It has been over 24 hours since I woke up yesterday morning, and I cannot think anymore."

"You look dead on your feet," Ewan said, not thinking. "I mean, you look tired. That probably wasn't the best phrase to use; sorry about that." Ewan grimaced; he hoped that Rylee didn't take offense to his off-handed comment.

"I knew what you meant. I am going to crash in your bed," Rylee replied. She really didn't care about silly vernacular right now, "Nobody would think to look for me here, and you're dead. This is the safest place we can be for now."

"Sleep well, Rylee," Ewan said with a hint of longing in his voice.

As Rylee walked into the bedroom, she saw Ewan attempt to open another drawer, only to swear in frustration when he couldn't. Maybe he would at least find something in the open to jog his memory.

RYLEE WOKE up a few hours later to her stomach grumbling. She stretched and looked around the room. Wow, Ewan really didn't bother to keep his room clean, Rylee thought as she took in her surroundings. She was too tired to notice before. Rylee got up and returned to the living room, where she saw more of the same mess. How can anyone live like this? She didn't want to judge Ewan, but as a medium, she picked up on the aura of a space more than ordinary people did.

"You are awake! Finally," Ewan seemed irritated, but Rylee had no idea why.

"What's wrong?" Rylee was concerned at Ewan's attitude; this place was supposed to be safe.

"I tried to start searching for answers, but I can't touch anything," Ewan whined; his irritation was less evident now and gave way to frustration.

"Oh! Spirits can't interact with the physical world in the same way." She was too tired to remember his futile attempts from the night before. Had he been trying all night? No wonder he was so frustrated. "I need to grab a snack before we start, but I promise, we will dig through everything here and find answers."

"Mr. Kildare always kept snacks and food around. He knew that I was broke most of the time. Go knock on his door, and he will definitely have some fresh fruit and crackers for you."

"Great," Rylee replied, and she did as Ewan told her.

Mr. Kildare did not disappoint. He gave her some grapes, a couple of apples, and crackers. He smiled and told her not to be a stranger, reminding her that any friend of Ewan's was a friend of his.

Now that Rylee had some food in her stomach, it was time to get to work. She sifted through some of the papers on his desk, organizing them by their dates the best they could. Ewan stopped her when she picked up a childish sketch.

"That's him," he whispered.

"Who?" Rylee asked, knowing that this was the first solid lead they had to go off of. Finally.

Ewan stared at the drawing. "He took me away from my parents. They were on drugs, and I was starving. He gave me a warm place to stay and fed me. He protected me, but something was terrifying about him," Ewan started to explain.

Rylee reached out to touch his hand out of instinct. She jumped back when she felt his hand under hers.

Ewan shrank away as well.

"I can touch you!" Rylee shrieked.

"No, really?" His words dripped with sarcasm. "This is weird; you are definitely not dead because you can touch things in the physical world. What is going on?"

Rylee started pacing across the bedroom, trying to make sense of what was going on right now. Why could she touch a spirit? She had to be missing something!

"Uncle Tars never explained anything, and my abilities didn't come to the surface until my parents died, so I never had the opportunity to ask them about this stuff. Gah! I feel so unprepared to do any of this," she continued to pace until Ewan caught her in his arms and held her tight.

"It is going to be okay, Rylee," Ewan tried to soothe her, "this just means that you are special; it isn't a bad thing."

Rylee didn't really agree, but there were more pressing matters. "Okay, you are right. Let's keep going," Rylee sighed. "How did you live like this? Everything is a mess?"

"I-I didn't." Ewan processed what it meant. "Someone must have broken in before we got here. They must have been looking for something. I swear, my apartment was never this messy when I was alive!"

They continued looking through the papers on his desk. Ewan remembered more about the mysterious figure. He took him away from his parents for his protection but scared the life out of him at the same time. Ewan recalled that once he went with this man, he never returned to school. He couldn't remember why.

"I remember asking why I couldn't see my friends anymore after a couple of weeks," Ewan said, looking at more drawings from his youth.

"Is this man Mr. B.G.?" Rylee asked, thinking about what she heard back at the shop. "Isn't he the one who had it out for all of those drug runners, dealers, and crime bosses?"

"Yes! One and the same! I can't believe I forgot that." Ewan gave Rylee a hug. "We really are making progress."

Rylee's heart hurt for Ewan's lost childhood. He had it worse from what he explained than she did; at least she was a teenager before she lost her parents. She was all too aware of how common drug use was in their city. With so many Powered individuals running around, those without them often felt weak. In rare cases, drug use could give someone the same powers as a medium, mind control abilities, or even the powers of a Reaper. Many desperate souls lost themselves to drugs trying to gain powers they never had.

"I don't remember anything," Ewan whispered. "There's so much I don't know. Did the man kill me? He's Mr. B.G., right? Did he do it? But he raised me?"

The hurt and confusion in his voice struck Rylee in the soul. She gently brushed her fingers against his arm. The action sent tingles through her fingertips and seemed to soothe Ewan.

As they continued to look through the papers and notebooks around Ewan's apartment, they found any excuse to touch. Whether it is a finger, the back of their hands, or interlocking their arms. They were playfully testing how far this phenomenon stretched. Ewan picked up a book without thinking while Rylee was running her fingers up and down his arm. He almost dropped it just as quickly when he realized what was happening.

"Rylee!" Ewan exclaimed. "When you touch me, it is like I am part of the physical world again. Look!" He picked up a book in one hand while touching her with his other.

Rylee was even more surprised at this revelation. She wished her uncle had told her more about her abilities. It would be helpful right about now to know what was going on and what was possible.

Why didn't Uncle Tars want me to be able to use my connection with the spirits? Why did he tell me to keep away? She wondered as they continued to look around.

Her uncle was always so cryptic when he spoke about her gift. All she could understand was that whatever caused him to keep things from her had something to do with her parents' deaths. She felt anger rising in her because she needed information and knew that calling her uncle was not a wise move right now. For all she knew, he could be involved with Mr. B.G. and feeding him any information she gave him.

"Ewan, this is so complicated! How am I supposed to help you when I don't even know about my own abilities?" Rylee slid down to the floor and rested her head in her hands.

Ewan crouched down next to her and stroked her hair. "Let's take advantage of this newfound ability of yours. Now we can both look through these papers and books; we will get through it twice as fast as long as we are touching in some way." Ewan smiled at the thought of keeping contact with Rylee. Whatever allowed them to touch, he was thankful for it. It wouldn't be fair to be in the presence of someone so sweet, kind, and beautiful and not be able to touch them.

"Yeah, okay. That's a good idea. We need to use this." Rylee sounded a little bit more confident as she allowed Ewan to pull her off the floor. "I think we have organized everything in here; let's go back to the living room and see what we can find there."

They were able to move through stacks of papers and documents much quicker now that they understood that there was a way to allow Ewan to interact with the physical world. Occasionally one of them would break contact, and whatever Ewan was holding would suddenly drop to the floor. It was frustrating when it was a piece of paper but downright startling when it was a book. They got better about staying in contact and began teasing each other with soft touches on their necks and faces that raised goose bumps.

They found more evidence that Mr. B.G. was controlling most of Ewan's life from the time he was a young boy up until he died. This man was a master at getting what he wanted; taking him down would not be easy. Rylee began to wonder if Mr. B.G. was powered himself. It was an awful thought that made their task even harder. It also became more and more apparent that he was likely the man threatening Rylee's life. The good news was they seemed to have a decent paper trail to follow that would help them understand some of Mr. B.G.'s patterns, but they still lacked any motive for wanting them dead.

Rylee was still processing everything that she had learned about her abilities when out of nowhere, Ewan picked her up and carried her to the couch. She gasped in surprise but found she liked it. It was exciting, thrilling, and something profound in her wanted to see how far it would go. Ewan held her close and went back to stroking her hair much like he was in the bedroom. He rubbed her back and dared to slip one hand up her shirt. When she didn't resist, he unhooked her bra to free her breasts.

Rylee only had a couple boyfriends before this. She felt she was still inexperienced, but she knew that Ewan's attention and touch felt good. She felt her bra release and slip away from her chest. His hands felt strong and soothing on her back. She didn't want him to have all the fun, so she leaned in and kissed him deeply while his hands were exploring her body.

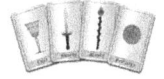

FIVE

Gold Mine

As they explored each other's' bodies, Rylee started to get hungry again. Still, she felt terrible that she kept bothering Mr. Kildare for food, and she certainly didn't want to stop Ewan. As the thought crossed her mind, and as if on cue, someone knocked on the door.

Rylee and Ewan both jumped at the sound. Rylee quickly fixed her clothing and crept to the door. She searched for anything that could be a weapon as she neared the door, settling on an old, dusty umbrella. Peering through the peephole, umbrella at the ready, she saw a smiling Mr. Kildare holding a large pot in his hands.

"Mr. Kildare!" Rylee exclaimed as she opened the door. "You surprised me!"

"I am so sorry to scare you, little lady," Mr. Kildare apologized. "I just thought that you might want some sausage and peppers for dinner tonight. It was one of my favorite things to cook for Ewan."

"Oh, that is so nice, Mr. Kildare, please come in," Rylee invited. "Let me grab plates, and we can eat. I would love to get to know you better."

Ewan guided her to the cabinet with plates and the drawer that held his silverware so Rylee didn't look out of place.

Mr. Kildare served Rylee and himself, and they sat down to eat. "You look like you need answers to a mystery, little lady," Mr. Kildare said. "Is there something I can do to help?"

Rylee was taken aback, she had no idea how Mr. Kildare knew she was looking for information while she was here, but it couldn't hurt to ask. "Mr. Kildare, Ewan mentioned that I should find some information here, but I can't seem to locate as much as I had hoped."

"Oh, well, that would make sense. Ewan mentioned having a safe place to store his most important items," Mr. Kildare replied. "He said something about not wanting his boss to know about it."

"You know, Ewan did mention that to me. I completely forgot. Did he ever tell you more about it?" Rylee asked, rolling with the punches.

Mr. Kildare chuckled. "You know our friend Ewan; he keeps everything close to his chest. He hasn't told me much. Something about keeping me safe in case things go bad."

"Of course, Mr. Kildare," Rylee replied. "I was just wondering if he happened to let slip a location. But I totally understand if he didn't tell you, mysterious as he tried to be."

"Well, he has visions," Mr. Kildare said after a brief pause. "He let it slip one day when he came home looking a bit rough. I invited him in for tea and helped him clean up. I am pretty sure he didn't want anyone to know about them, though," Mr. Kildare added, looking somewhat disappointed with himself for revealing it.

"You're damn right! I didn't want anyone to know about them, old man," Ewan said indignantly.

Rylee had to hold back a laugh. She knew that Ewan wasn't really mad at Mr. Kildare; mostly, he was frustrated at this whole situation. Rylee finished eating and placed the dishes in the sink. "Thank you so much for this amazing dinner; I can see why Ewan likes it so much," Rylee said with a smile at Ewan's neighbor as he got ready to go back to his apartment.

"Keep the leftovers, little lady. You and Ewan will have a nice dinner waiting for you." Mr. Kildare had a sly, knowing grin on his face as he left.

Rylee tried not to rush to close the door behind him too quickly, but they needed to know where this storage place was and how to get into it. They promptly began searching for a key around the apartment. Just as Rylee started to get frustrated, she noticed a picture that hung on the wall in a strange location. She took it down and found a compartment with a small envelope inside with a key. The envelope had a logo for one of the storage facilities across town.

"Bingo!" Rylee yelled, showing the key to Ewan. "Let's go!"

///

"OH, THANK HEAVENS!" Ewan said when they opened the storage unit.

Rylee watched as relief washed over Ewan's face. He may not have remembered, but it was clear that he was glad to have found it. Rylee felt part of that herself and intertwined her hand in his, feeling a spark of joy at her touch.

Inside were stacks and stacks of journals. They must

have been there for years; some of them were over a decade old. Ewan had been meticulous about storing and hiding these, even putting the unit under a fake name. The effort suggested he wanted to hide but preserve them. They were important.

Rylee grabbed a stack of journals and notebooks and settled on the floor. Since nobody knew about this storage space, it was as safe a place as there could be. They could pause to arm herself with as much knowledge as possible. She hoped that she wouldn't come across her name or her parents' names in any of these journals. Still, she couldn't help but wonder if Ewan saw a vision about the car accident all those years ago or knew who caused it. Would these journals unlock a mystery that Rylee hadn't even known about 48 hours ago?

The journals were filled with details about every one of Ewan's visions. Some talked about the future and its implications; others were classified information about rival gangs or politicians.

"I wasn't using this against people, was I?" Ewan said.

Rylee gave his hand a squeeze.

They read for hours. Each journal created more questions than it answered. Rylee noticed that they all had something written in code in the margins. The more she studied it, the more she realized that it was really just two different codes that decorated each page's top corners. It was not in any code she knew, and it didn't come up in any of her books that talked about codes and people who had visions.

Ewan couldn't remember either, but he kept reading through the notebooks with the classified information. He tried to decipher what the difference was between the information on pages with each of the codes. The silence grew heavy between them; all that could be heard was the rustling of pages as they each looked for clues.

"I've got it!" Ewan shouted, causing Rylee to nearly jump out of her skin.

"Damn it, Ewan!" Rylee hissed at him, trying to get her heart rate back down. "Don't scare me like that!"

"Sorry, Rylee," Ewan said sheepishly, "but I figured it out. I figured out what the code is!"

"Are you going to share with the class or just keep shouting to watch me jump again?" Rylee tried to keep the frustration out of her voice, but she was on edge.

"Okay, so read these two pages," Ewan pushed the notebook into her hand, "do you see it? Do you see why they have different symbols?"

Rylee studied the pages Ewan was pointing to, but nothing was clicking. She was just as lost as she had been. She raised her eyebrow at Ewan. "I have no idea, man, just tell me, please."

"This symbol here means 'not for B.G.,' and this one here means 'for B.G.,'" he explained as if it should make perfect sense to her.

"I am still lost, Ewan; please fill in the gaps," Rylee urged.

"I was collecting information from what I can tell. B.G. wanted me to keep notes on different people inside and outside of his organization." Ewan was animated and jabbering. "But I went further than he asked. I gathered more information for myself as well. I knew more than I probably should have."

"He trusted you," Rylee said as she pieced together what he was saying, "but why? You were just a kid when he found you, and these notebooks and journals seem to start shortly after that. Why would he trust a nine-year-old with this kind of information?" Rylee had even more questions now. When did Ewan get his powers? Was he acting of his own free will?

"I have no clue, Rylee, I really don't know," Ewan sighed. "I am just starting to piece all of this together now. I wish it made more sense. I really do! I wish I'd had a normal childhood and none of these stupid visions!" He buried his face in his hands.

Rylee wrapped her arm around his shoulders. She wanted to make him feel better. She wanted to be able to provide a safe space for him. It seemed like he never had that; first, his parents, who were too cracked out to even notice he was gone, then Mr. B.G. took him in and used him for who knows what! He just needed someone to show him love, someone to show him that there was good to be seen in this world. It broke her heart that she couldn't be that for him while he was alive.

Ewan melted into Rylee's embrace and just wanted to stop all of his pain. He wanted to stay within her grasp forever, but they had work to do. Ewan shifted enough to let Rylee know it was time to get back to work, but he still kept contact with her so he could continue to interact with the physical world. He wished he understood why that was happening, but he was just going to take advantage of it for now.

They continued reading the journals and notebooks, trying to piece together the story of Ewan's life, when Rylee stumbled upon some passages that might be about her parents. It is hard to tell; they were never mentioned by name, but the timing did fall right before their accident. It seemed to discuss events that occurred near the family store.

"Ewan, there is something here, but important bits seem to have been redacted." She ran her fingers over a few big white spaces.

"Why would I redact something in my own journals?" Ewan studied the pages that Rylee pointed out to him. "Whatever I used to remove these bits of information must have been impressive. Look, there aren't even any indents from my pen like on the rest of the page."

Rylee was trying to understand why this one entry would have redacted information when all of these other notebooks and journals contained such terrible details about people. What could have made Ewan feel the need to cover something so thoroughly? What could be that bad? She wanted to think that her parents were good upstanding citizens; she didn't want to believe that they had anything to do with the likes of Mr. B.G. Was Uncle Tarsizio the good egg in the family? She didn't like where these thoughts were going, but she knew that it was important. She tucked that notebook into her bag to use later.

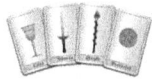

SIX

The Most Important Notebook

RYLEE CONTINUED TO LOOK THROUGH THE NOTEBOOKS and journals. She watched Ewan's handwriting become neater and more legible as he grew older. However, it looked as though he never went back to school. She saw his motivations change from pure loyalty to questioning uncertainty. Rylee read details she probably shouldn't have about his past. She felt her affections for him growing as she continued. There was still something bothering her, however. She needed to understand why Ewan couldn't remember anything he had written down. There was one question burning in her head; she couldn't ignore it anymore.

"Ewan, do you think that Mr. B.G. was using you for your visions?" she finally asked him. She didn't want to hurt him, but it just kept coming up in the various things she was reading that made her feel that Mr. B.G. was up to more than they could see right now.

Ewan stared at her. "I-I think you are right. I don't remember any of this," Ewan responded. He then let a string of expletives fly like Rylee had never heard before.

"Did he have me in a trance or something? How did he control me? Is that the only reason he took me away from my parents when I was a kid?"

"I don't know exactly how it is done, but I heard Uncle Tars talking to someone about doing just that to some kids when I had just started working at the shop after my parents died," Rylee sighed. "Apparently, it is pretty common for these crime bosses to 'adopt' special kids and use them to get the information they needed and wanted from various sources."

"Why?" Ewan cried. "My stupid parents had to be so hopped up on drugs to not even notice I was gone! I hate them!"

Rylee wanted to cry. None of this was fair. It seems that the rumors she heard from her uncle were true. It was bittersweet to know more about what Ewan's link to Mr. B.G. was and why he didn't remember anything. On the one hand, it was good because it gave them something to go off of, but on the other, Rylee could see how much Ewan was hurting as he put the pieces together.

"Oh, Ewan, I am so sorry. There might even be more to that story that we don't know, sweetie; they might not have been on drugs. Right now, we really just don't know. It is completely possible that they loved you and cared for you, and Mr. B.G. meddled with their memories too so he could take you away," Rylee tried to reason with him.

Just as Rylee was trying to comfort Ewan and figure out their next move, Ewan got a faraway look on his face. Rylee deduced that he was having a vision, and likely not a happy one. She watched as Ewan slowly came back to the present and waited for him to fill her in. He looked at her in a panic.

"Rylee! He has one of my notebooks! This is a nightmare. I need it back, now!"

"Ewan, why do you need it so badly? We have so many of them here to get information from." Rylee didn't understand why he was so panicked. Of course, it wasn't ideal for Mr. B.G. to have one of his notebooks, but for him to be this desperate didn't make sense to her. Going anywhere near Mr. B.G. without a solid plan seemed risky and unnecessary.

"Rylee, I wish I knew, but I just know that I need this notebook back from him! It feels like a life-and-death situation. Please, Rylee!" Ewan begged.

Rylee still didn't understand it, but seeing his desperation grow and the panic nearly boils over, she knew that she needed to do this for him.

"This is probably way riskier than I can even fathom, but, for you, Ewan, okay. Where did you see him? Where does he have your notebook?" Rylee asked.

Ewan's panic began to ease slightly as Rylee agreed to help him out. He gave her the directions to the pizza place that was probably a few miles from the storage unit. "Rylee, thank you, I know this is dangerous for you. I just know that getting this notebook back is crucial," Ewan told her. "If we leave now, we should still be able to catch him. I couldn't tell how long he stayed at this pizza joint."

Rylee grabbed her things that she had brought to the storage locker, checking that her crystal was still clear and close to her heart. She grabbed a couple of other journals and notebooks that seemed to have important information that they could use. She stashed them with the ones that seemed to hold the secrets about her parents that she longed to understand.

"Ewan, let's go. I don't want to get all the way there and miss him. Are you ready to face Mr. B.G.?" she asked, trying to appear brave.

"Yeah, I'm ready," he said.

Rylee gathered there was more behind the words but wasn't sure how to ask. The man did control his life for over a decade. It had to be a tricky situation.

Rylee locked up, and they snuck away from the storage place. Rylee hoped and prayed that nobody saw them. There was a lot more information in that locker that she wanted to look through. She tucked the key away in a secret pocket in her bag, just to be safe. She had a bad feeling about what they were about to walk into, but she couldn't let Ewan know how nervous she actually was. She stayed off the main streets for nearly the entire adventure, from the storage place to the pizza place. They stopped a couple of blocks away so Rylee could catch her breath before facing this mystery man.

Rylee psyched herself up to face Mr. B.G. and try to get this notebook back. She snuck into the pizza place and froze as she realized that Mr. B.G. wasn't alone. There must have been eight or more men sitting around Mr. B.G. looking menacing. He had a dark suit on that highlighted his muscular physique. His eyes that were probably once beautiful looked cold and distant now. His black hair was slicked back away from his face. Rylee was terrified. Ewan gently touched her arm, reminding her that they are in this together. She took a deep breath and scanned the space; one of the thugs has Ewan's notebook and is reading it to the group.

Well, that complicates things, Rylee, though. She stood there a few minutes longer and realized that what he was reading was about her.

Ewan seemed to realize that at the same time as Rylee and let another string of expletives escape, only Rylee could hear. They needed to get this notebook now! Hopefully, there were still things that they hadn't learned about her that they could avoid them knowing.

"Rylee, do you think you can focus enough to make it so I can interact with the physical world while we aren't touching?" Ewan asked. He needed to be able to help, but if they had to be touching, he couldn't get in and out without putting Rylee in more danger, something he had no intention of doing if he could avoid it.

"I can try," Rylee said with a shaky voice. "I need you to distract them. I have a plan, sort of."

Rylee held Ewan's hand and said a prayer under her breath. Focusing her energy on him, she tried to draw him more into their world. There were, after all, spirits that could interact with physical objects. It was a rare skill that the spirit usually acquired after years of refusing to move on.

The longer she focused, the more she felt Ewan's presence. She didn't let go until she felt Ewan as part of the physical world and less a part of the spirit world. This had to work! They separated, and Ewan appeared to be more solid than not, which was a good sign.

"Are you ready to break this party up?" her voice was shaking even more now. If she couldn't get in and out without being seen, she was undoubtedly a dead girl walking.

Ewan started to creep up to the group of men, slowly and carefully. When he was close enough, he began causing mayhem; dumping drinks on people's heads, upending tables, flipping the chairs the men occupied, and worse.

This seemed to be enough of a cover for Rylee to sneak in and do what she needed to. In all of the chaos, the notebook had fallen to the ground, and she was able to grab it off the floor. For once, her small stature was a benefit. She tucked it away and skirted out of the fray of things.

"Rylee, hurry up; they won't stay distracted long. We need to move!" Ewan hurried her along.

The restaurant felt enormous as she started to get away. She nearly made it to the door as Mr. B.G. began to regain control of the room. They got all the tables and chairs righted and dried off from the soda that was spilled everywhere. They were all furious, but they were falling into step with Mr. B.G. again. Rylee had one hand on the door as she heard shouting from behind her.

"That's her," one of the men yelled. "Somebody grab her!"

SEVEN

Facing the Enemy

RYLEE SPRINTED DOWN THE STREETS WITH EWAN'S spectral form behind her. Her pursuers were close, but she hoped she was faster. She was certainly better dressed for running through the streets, thanks to her sneakers and leggings. They, meanwhile, had stuffy suits and dress shoes. On the very edge of her senses, she picked up guilt and worry from Ewan. She had to focus on something else, however. His emotions would only distract her.

"We need to get away from here, now!" Rylee shouted as she tried to get her bearings.

She weaved through the streets, trying to take the most convoluted path possible to make it harder to follow them. Her heart was racing with adrenaline, and very few thoughts were connecting in her head.

Where can they go? Have all of their safe spots been compromised? We need to put more space between them and us. The thoughts were dancing in and out of her brain, but she didn't have answers to the questions she was asking.

She felt someone behind her as she banked around

another corner. She had no idea how they were able to keep up with her twists and turns. She barely evaded his grasp as she vaulted over a fence. She heard something fall behind her. Perhaps Ewan had knocked something over to block the path? Or maybe the man fell trying to jump the fence?

She needed more space, someplace she could hide. That fence would only slow him down for a short while. She knew that a few of her medium friends lived in this area, but she wasn't sure if she could trust them; she wasn't sure if she could trust anyone.

The guy following her did not seem perturbed by the chase or the strange path she followed. Every time she created extra distance, he appeared to be back in hot pursuit of her in the time it took her to cross a few blocks.

"This is insane. Why can he track me so well?" Rylee whined.

"Powered, maybe?" Ewan suggested. It was odd hearing his voice so normal. He was dead, so he wasn't out of breath from running. He was just there. He floated alongside Rylee, keeping contact with her to gain some physical presence.

Rylee used her powers to connect with the spirits that lingered in the area to help create physical and spiritual space between her and her pursuer. I need help, she shouted mentally into the spirit world, touching her mind to other spirits.

The results felt slow, given the situation, but the spirits responded. One by one, they flung objects, reached for his clothes or limbs, or blocked his path. Those that weren't physical enough to stop him slowed him as their chilling grip and presence drained energy from him.

With her powers and agitation, they were able to interact with the physical world enough to give them a big lead off this guy. This allowed them to escape to Ewan's apartment and slip inside unnoticed.

"We are not safe here. They are going to figure out I know about your journals and come looking for me in any place you have been known to spend time," Rylee gasped as she caught her breath. "I just need to make sure I have all of my things, and we need to leave here."

"Rylee, I am so sorry. I should have listened to you. We should never have gone to that pizza place." Ewan's voice sounded anguished.

"No, Ewan, you were right; we needed to go and get that notebook. Now we can figure out why Mr. B.G. wants me dead," Rylee reassured him as she raced around the apartment, gathering the last of her things that managed to end up sprawled everywhere.

"We need to get out of here and make a plan. I think Mr. Kildare will let you stay there for a little bit to make a plan," Ewan reasoned.

"How much can I tell him?" Rylee wondered.

"It doesn't matter anymore. Just do what you have to do to stay out of sight. Depending on how well he takes, the fact that you are being chased by the city's biggest crime boss will determine how much you can share. But let's go!" Ewan was exasperated and terrified.

Rylee closed his door and locked it. Although she wasn't sure why she bothered, she figured Mr. B.G.'s men would be there any minute breaking the door down. She knocked on Mr. Kildare's door urgently.

"Miss Rylee, are you okay?" Mr. Kildare was visibly concerned.

"Please can I come inside, now!" Rylee urged.

"Yes, yes, please do," Mr. Kildare stepped aside, "come in, sweetie, and tell me what's wrong."

As the door closed behind them, Rylee heard footsteps

in the hallway. She motioned for Mr. Kildare to be very quiet as she looked through the peephole. The man who had been following her busted down Ewan's door without a second thought. Rylee was shaking, knowing that if they had taken just one minute longer in the apartment, she would be dead for sure. The man's heavy, angry steps echoed through the tiny apartment hallway as he searched the rooms. He left after a brief amount of time, realizing the apartment was empty. Rylee knew they could never return there. They would be watching. She slid down the door and buried her face in her hands as she hit the floor. Ewan wrapped his arms around her, trying to calm her down.

"What is going on, little lady? Who was that man who broke down Ewan's door?" Mr. Kildare asked as he helped Rylee up and got her settled in the living room. He drew his curtains even though he was sure nobody could see into his apartment from the streets.

Rylee launched into an explanation of everything that had occurred since the séance on Saturday. She even told him that Ewan has been with her this entire time as a spirit and helped her figure out why Mr. B.G. was after her, and she was helping him piece together the secrets of his past.

"We just escaped from Mr. B.G.'s thugs after grabbing this notebook. That is why that guy broke down Ewan's door. This notebook contains the information Ewan wrote about me before he died. This is likely the answer to so many questions," Rylee explained. "We have more of his journals and notebooks here that we haven't gone through yet, but we are in serious danger right now."

"Oh! Rylee, I am so sorry, my sweet girl. This is terrible. I want to help, Ewan was very dear to me, and I am heartbroken that this vicious man killed him. We will figure this out," Mr. Kildare said matter-of-factly.

"Mr. Kildare, Ewan, and I never meant to get you involved in all of this. We just had nowhere else to turn." Rylee was on the verge of tears.

"Never you mind that!" Mr. Kildare assured. "Ewan was like a grandson to me, and if you are helping him, then I want to help you. First, let's get you some tea for your nerves. When was the last time you ate something?"

Rylee knew they had dinner together the night before but couldn't remember eating since. Had it been nearly a full day since she put anything in her body? That was very unlike her, especially when she was using her powers.

"Umm, I think it was at dinner last night when you came over," she replied sheepishly.

"Well, let me whip something up, and we can figure out what is going on in this crazy town." Mr. Kildare jumped into action.

Rylee could hear him banging around in the kitchen. She was grateful for his quick acceptance and offer to help. Still, she also needed a moment to grasp everything that was happening. She could barely believe it. How were they going to bring down the most robust crime network in the city? We are two people and one spirit; they have hundreds of connections. The odds indeed were not in their favor.

Mr. Kildare returned with sandwiches and tea for Rylee; he didn't like that she skipped meals. "Miss Rylee, can I ask you a few questions so I can make sure I am up to speed?" he asked, trying not to pry but desperate to understand.

"Um, sure?" Rylee shrugged. "I will answer what I can, but there is a lot that I still don't understand."

"Thank you, darling," Mr. Kildare began. "So you are a medium, and you can actually interact with the spirit world?"

"Yes, I can speak to spirits who have not yet fully

53

crossed over, and I can get glimpses of those that have. I am still training my power; it only began after my parents died, so I didn't have them to guide me through the beginning years," Rylee explained in between bites. She didn't realize how hungry she was until she started eating.

"I am so sorry for your loss. Does Mr. B.G. know that you are a medium? Is it common knowledge?" He continued.

"I don't know who knows about my abilities outside of Uncle Tars and a couple of friends who are mediums as well," Rylee said. "But now that you mention it, Mr. B.G. must know, why else would he be trying to kill me? My uncle isn't very forthcoming with information with me, and he sometimes runs with some sketchy crowds."

Ewan sighed. He rested his hand on her thigh, and he began to manifest into a physical form on Mr. Kildare's couch. Neither Rylee nor Ewan noticed until Mr. Kildare gasped, nearly falling backward on his chair.

"Ewan!" he exclaimed. "You're here!" He didn't know what else to say, he knew his neighbor was dead, but here he was sitting on the couch next to Rylee as she explained how she interacts with the spirit world.

"Oh! Sorry, Mr. Kildare," Ewan apologized before he explained what was happening. "We learned that I could touch Rylee, and that lets me interact with the physical world."

"I can see that! You look just like you did the last time I saw you. Are you ever going to brush your messy, blond hair?" Mr. Kildare smiled and regained his friendly ambiance. "You could have led with that one, little lady." He smiled at Rylee to reassure her that she was still safe with him while it had startled him.

"Right, sorry, Mr. Kildare," Rylee was slightly embarrassed that she forgot to mention that to him. She leaned back against the couch, and Ewan settled in with his arm around her shoulders. All Rylee wanted was to feel safe, so there was work to be done, but for now, she just relished the warmth and protection that Ewan provided. She was ready to fall asleep in his arms.

"Rylee, you have had a long day. Do you want to take a nap before we start trying to bring down a crime syndicate?" Mr. Kildare offered softly. "I can bring you a blanket and give you two some privacy if you want."

"Mr. Kildare, that sounds perfect. Thank you," Rylee responded. She needed to allow herself to be taken care of for a little while before facing the impossible task that lay ahead of her.

EIGHT

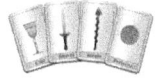

Haunted by the Past

WHEN RYLEE WOKE UP FROM HER NAP, SHE SMELLED dinner. It took a moment for her to remember where she was and what was going on.

"How long was I asleep?" she asked, afraid to know the answer.

"A few hours," Mr. Kildare said from the kitchen. "Dinner will be ready soon."

Rylee's stomach grumbled as if to put a finer point on exactly how long she had been asleep. "Why didn't one of you wake me? We have so much to do, and we have no idea if this building is safe or what Mr. B.G. is up to!" Rylee was in a tizzy and couldn't decide what was most important right now.

"Rylee, look at me," Ewan said in a calm and quiet voice, "remember what we talked about when we first got to my apartment Sunday morning?"

Rylee stared at him like he had three heads. Why would she remember something inconsequential that was said three days ago? "Of course I don't. I have been busy being chased by people who want to kill me!" she growled.

"You still need your sleep to be useful in this endeavor. Remember, you took a nap when we got there, and I couldn't touch anything," Ewan was incredibly talented at grounding her. He stroked her hair and held her close.

It was as if he poked a hole in her balloon. The fight was slowly leaking out of her. She took a deep breath and nodded; she really did need the sleep she got, especially after they had. She felt his gorgeous blue eyes staring into her soul. "Sorry, Ewan," she said. "I am just so scared!"

"I know, sweetie," Ewan told her, "we are going to figure this out. After you have something to eat, we can start diving deeper into these journals, I promise." He kissed her head again and squeezed her tight before encouraging her to get up and have dinner with Mr. Kildare.

Rylee ate the excellent dinner Mr. Kildare prepared. She tried to savor it, but she was still numb from this whole crazy week. When are we going to catch a break? Every time we think we have made progress, things get ten times worse. She pondered over her spaghetti and meat sauce.

When Rylee finished, Mr. Kildare cleared their plates and refilled her glass of juice. She was still a bit pale for his liking, but he sent her back into the living room to start looking through the journals and notebooks with Ewan while he finished cleaning the kitchen. Mr. Kildare assured them he would help soon, but he needed to keep his apartment clean as well. Some things couldn't be sacrificed until absolutely necessary.

Rylee settled back onto the couch with Ewan and picked up the journal with the earliest date. It talked about how Mr. B.G. used Ewan to help find other kids with powers through his visions. By the time Ewan turned ten, eight more kids had been 'adopted' by Mr. B.G. Ewan had been one of the first taken in. Still, there was a constant flow of recruits that Mr. B.G. had Ewan train and watched over. This explained why Ewan never returned to school. He was a part-time babysitter and a full-time workhorse for Mr. B.G.

The following journal they picked up talked about the children's training and how brutal it had been. Ewan often had to hold the younger children as they cried after every training session to help them fall asleep. He learned how to tough it out and not let Mr. B.G. see any weakness in him.

One day, Ewan had seen one of the youngest recruits who must have been no older than five or six die during training; that broke him more than he wanted to admit. He was around sixteen, and from that day, he decided that he would get out of there and help as many of the kids as possible. Ewan continued to work for Mr. B.G. and do his dirty work, even though he hated it. Still, he started to keep separate journals at that point because he was gathering more information than Mr. B.G. asked him to collect. He planned to use it to escape and bring the whole gang down.

He continued to help the younger kids through the training and comforted them when they missed their parents or friends. He found an entry about someone that joined as an adult. Ewan always wondered what would make someone with powers want to join Mr. B.G. willingly. But this guy was a tracer. He was able to find people as long as he had seen their faces.

"This is him. This is the guy that was following you," Ewan said, trying not to yell and startle Rylee in her fragile state. "Look, he is the right age, and it explains why you couldn't shake him despite the winding path you took."

"I don't know if that makes me feel better or worse," Rylee whimpered. "It sounds like I will never be safe as long as he is out there."

What she didn't say was the thought that truly scared her. *He is probably playing cards on the other side of that door, just waiting for me to step out so he can make sure I am killed in the most brutal way possible. He wants to lull me into a false sense of security.*

"No, Rylee, there is more," Ewan told her, "most people didn't evade him for long, so it felt like he could find people no matter what, but if somebody was out of his sight for more than an hour, they might as well be a ghost. He needed to keep a constant watch on someone to be able to find them if they ran. You are safe; it has been over eight hours since he saw you last." He watched Rylee breathe a sigh of relief with a soft, loving smile.

Now that Rylee had calmed down a bit, they returned to the journals and notebooks. All of the reading was slowly bringing Ewan's memory back. He would stop to comment about something he remembered or hunt for a journal.

Rylee had her nose buried in one notebook in particular. "Ewan, look at this," she said, "there is an address, and it talks about rescuing the recruits."

"Oh! Rylee, yes! I think I wrote that maybe a week before I died, time is still a bit fuzzy," Ewan pondered.

"Well, now is as good a time as any. It is the only concrete piece of information we have to act on."

Rylee saw no point in waiting. These kids were in danger now. She had no intention of letting Mr. B.G. use them as pawns anymore. It was about more than her life now. She started gathering her things before Ewan or Mr. Kildare could respond. She organized all of the notebooks and journals strewn across the coffee table, floor, and couch. She was ready to bring them all with her when Mr. Kildare gently touched her hand.

"Rylee, take a moment to breathe," Mr. Kildare said

softly. "You can leave these notebooks and journals here. I will not look at them without you, but I have a safe place where you can be sure nobody will find them."

Rylee stared at him for a few moments. I trust this man, but this is all of the information we have about Mr. B.G. Can we really go to war without it? What if something happens to Mr. Kildare because someone thinks he has information? Will they torture him to find out? Will he cave and hand all of this over? Thoughts were racing through her mind faster than she could process them, but in the end, she agreed to leave the notebooks and journals with him. There were just two that she needed to keep; one that had information about her parents and the one they rescued from the pizza place that was all about her.

Ewan had been strangely quiet through this whole discussion. "Rylee, you know once we get to this address, we are declaring war on Mr. B.G. That will only end in one of two ways, and both involve death, either yours or his."

"I know, let's go. There is no time to waste." Rylee put on a brave face, grabbed the bag she packed, and opened the door.

Nobody was in the hallway; no one alive was in the hallway anyway. Many ghosts were lingering about, their incorporeal forms emerging from the walls to peer at her.

"Ewan, I think the spirit world is rising up to help us. There are more and more spirits that are appearing and speaking to me," Rylee said, giving them a slight wave.

"I can see them," Ewan whispered. "This is a good thing, right?"

"Yes," Rylee responded.

Even the ghosts around them nodded. They were of varying ages. Some were very young, others around her age, give or take a couple years, others were older still.

Some had sweet faces with kind eyes, while others wore scars and cold, steely eyes.

They had an uneventful trip to the address in the notebook, but every few blocks jogged Ewan's memory more. He was finally able to control it and process what he was remembering. They were both slightly tense, but they arrived at the address and found cover in a dark alley.

"We need to enter through the side door. It is the only one that doesn't have cameras. It is mostly obscured, so only Mr. B.G.'s men know it is there," Ewan remembered.

"Let's do it." Rylee snuck around to the side that Ewan described, and they quickly approached the building.

The building was an old complex, probably a factory. Rylee wasn't sure on the specific purpose of it in the past, but it looked like Mr. B.G. had turned it into barracks for the children under his control. Cameras and guards were scattered around the building. Getting in wouldn't be easy.

"Luckily, I'm already dead," Ewan said with a wink. "I'll help you get in."

Rylee was both irritated and amused that he could find some humor in the situation. "How?"

One of the other ghosts chimed in with a voice like the cracking of static, "I'm good with electronics. I can help you get by the cameras."

Rylee didn't really want to ask why he was good with them. Perhaps it was something in life. It also could have been the reason his voice sounded the way it did. "I'd appreciate it, thank you."

The staticky ghost disabled cameras and motion sensors while Ewan guided her around the guards. The other spirits helped them gather the other children. Most of the powered kids could interact with the dead in some way and were quick to listen to their supportive voices. The ghosts of former gang members were all too happy to search for information and navigate the complex for weaknesses.

With so many children, it was hard to keep track of everyone. Rylee was able to manifest Ewan once more, but even with all of them and the ghosts, there were too many to watch at all times. The older children did their best, but everyone was scared. They were near the final exit when the alarm tripped. The staticky ghost from before moved on to disable another motion sensor just as one of the younger children doubled back.

"Ewan, let's GO!" Rylee urged as Ewan closed the door and repositioned the shrubbery that hid it. "B.G. knows we are here. We need to get away before we put all of these kids in more danger."

NINE

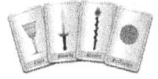

Escaping to the Ranch

EWAN AND RYLEE ROUNDED UP THE KIDS. THE YOUNGER children were frightened, clutching stuffed animals, small blankets, or each other for moral support and comfort. The older children were visibly nervous but quick to obey orders that were given. Too bad Rylee didn't have any orders for them. They didn't exactly plan much out before they began the mass breakout. Rylee racked her brain for ways to protect the kids and position themselves where they can work to continue taking Mr. B.G. down.

"Rylee!" Ewan gasped. "I know how we'll get out!"

Rylee nodded, assuming Ewan had a vision about it. She was desperate. The ghostly gang members may have been eager to hold off their living enemies, but they weren't able to do much.

"There is a bus that is parked on the corner two blocks away," Ewan began. "Rylee, you are going to drive it, and we will get somewhere safe. It's a ranch way outside of town. I don't know why, but I know it's safe there."

Ewan waved for everyone to follow him while Rylee

took her place at the back of the group. She didn't want anyone to fall behind or double back again.

At Rylee's command, the spirits formed a kind of barrier between the building and Rylee's group. Some of the spirits, the ones that had been dead longer, could reach her easier. They would be able to tell her if anyone was coming. Somehow, the crazy combination of medium, powered children, and dozens of ghosts worked. They reached the bus.

"Quickly, everyone on board," Rylee urged.

The children scurried onto the bus, some of them daring to look back through the windows. Rylee felt a pang of guilt. They didn't look mistreated, and this may have been the only home some of them ever knew.

"Under the third row of seats," Ewan said.

Rylee scrambled to the third row and reached under the chair. Just as Ewan had said, there was a hidden key tucked neatly into a tear in the chair's fabric.

Ewan and the older kids helped the younger ones get settled, taking great care to protect the stuffed animals and blankets. Rylee wondered if Ewan ever cuddled a stuffed animal or felt safe under a soft, warm blanket. Mr. B.G. stole all of that when he took Ewan away from his family; from that moment on, Ewan was forced to be an adult and take on real responsibilities.

Rylee caught Ewan watching a young woman comfort a young child. The child couldn't have been more than three. She had Shirley Temple-style curls in her beautiful red hair, and freckles dotted her button nose. She sobbed into the arms of the young woman. Rylee wasn't entirely sure about the girl's age, probably around the same age as her. Although she was sitting clutching the little girl, it was evident that she was more than a few inches taller than Rylee. Her hair was a slightly darker shade of red than the little girl's, but it was nearly as curly. How cruel was Mr. B.G. to steal this sweet child's innocence?

Rylee had never driven a bus before. It seemed more complicated than her uncle's rusted old truck. As she drove, it wasn't too different from some of the delivery trucks from the store. Sure she didn't drive them much, but parking them still gave her a feel for the controls.

"Rylee, you are doing great! Just keep following my directions. It isn't much farther," Ewan encouraged. "You know, I am starting to get more of my memories back every moment. I remember wanting to escape for years. I knew Mr. B.G. was manipulating me. That is why I started keeping the different journals. I was trying to gather information to get out of there. But I didn't want to leave all of the kids behind." Ewan looked at all the children in the bus before adding, "They were basically my adopted children. I couldn't leave them."

"Oh, Ewan, I am so sorry you had to live like that," Rylee murmured.

Her love for him was growing by the moment. She knew from what she read in his notebooks that he didn't want to help Mr. B.G. once Ewan figured out how he was being used, but the fact that he didn't want to leave the other kids vulnerable made her want to cry. Why was such a sweet boy treated so harshly? He could have been like the others who grew up and continued the tradition, but instead, he wanted better; he wanted to save people, she thought as she drove.

"Rylee, turn here. There is a roadblock up ahead; if we hit that, we are dead," Ewan told her in a quiet but firm voice.

"Got it," Rylee deftly turned down the next street and avoided the roadblock.

"You are a natural at driving this thing, hun." Ewan smiled as she swerved around the corners.

Rylee wasn't sure she believed him, but she liked hearing the praise and the joy in his voice. She was so comfortable and relaxed around him, although it hadn't been very long. And she got the sense that he felt the same way. She found herself wondering if they could be together physically and permanently, but the thought made her ache. He was still dead, even if he could manifest temporarily.

"Rylee, I think that you are the answer," Ewan blurted out.

"To what?" Rylee was caught off guard.

"You have always been the most important person in my life, even if neither of us remembers why, and because of this, you are how I will break free of Mr. B.G. for good!"

They left the city, and the landscape changed drastically. The office buildings and apartments were replaced with open land and houses with yards. The suburban area looked welcoming on the surface, but it still made Rylee uneasy for some reason. Luckily they traveled down side streets and didn't encounter any traffic. The landscape changed again; fields of crops dotted the sides of the road.

As they got farther from the city, the kids started to relax. They pointed out the cows and horses they saw on the farms; these were animals they had never seen outside of books and television. There were even some goats and chickens on a few of the farms. Ewan couldn't help but smile as he watched the children they rescued experience childhood for the first time. The older kids helped the younger ones as they identified the animals they saw and made all different sounds.

Rylee enjoyed the giggles and squeals that came from the back of the bus. She knew that she was doing something good. She saw the anguish on Ewan's face as he continued to tell her about some of his experiences as one of Mr. B.G.'s Powered People. Some of the more complex stories reminded them of why they were doing this; he told her about one particularly intense day of training that occurred a few years after Mr. B.G. took him.

"I must have been around thirteen; I started growing facial hair, and my voice was constantly squeaking. I hated everything about myself. Mr. B.G. decided to use that against me. He wanted to make sure I knew that, without him, my days were numbered. He put me in a dark room with a video playing; it showed some of the most brutal interrogation scenes I could imagine. I wanted to look away, but he had secured my head to the chair.

"It wasn't until the video was about halfway through that I started recognizing people. They were people I had found for Mr. B.G. I remember it made me want to be sick. I never intended for my visions to hurt people. I think Mr. B.G. wanted to use my self-hatred and the interrogations as a way to stop me from escaping. What would happen if I ran? Who would I be? I had been seen around some of these people shortly before their disappearances, but Mr. B.G. kept me away from the cops.

"Without his protection, I would surely rot in jail, or worse. These people had connections to the other crime families and gangs that ruled the city; I was sure that I wouldn't last a day on my own. I think that is what broke me for a long time. I was just another one of his soldiers that needed to fall in line." His voice shook as a shiver ran down his spine.

Ewan was on the verge of tears when Rylee made the last turn before pulling up to the ranch that Ewan described to her earlier. She parked the bus and asked the children to stay put for a few moments. Rylee motioned for

Ewan to follow her. She left the older kids in charge before closing the door behind them.

"Ewan, you are not responsible for what Mr. B.G. made you do. He had complete control over you and made sure you couldn't leave without fearing for your life. I don't hold any of this against you, I promise. I love you, Ewan." Rylee wrapped Ewan in her arms and kissed him deeply.

He was stunned by her proclamation, especially after everything he had shared on their drive. "Rylee," he whispered, breaking away from her kiss. "I love you, too."

They held each other for a moment longer, but they had work to do. They had to get the kids settled in and make them feel safe. Hopefully, Ewan was right, and this was a safe space. Rylee couldn't bear the thought of putting these kids in any more danger. Safety was not something these children had known for a long time, and it was time to reintroduce the concept to them, once and for all.

TEN

Settling In

"Ewan, stay here, keep your eyes peeled for anything unusual. I'm going to see if anyone is here," Rylee told him, squeezing his hands before she left him.

She found the ranch house a bit off the road and softly knocked on the door. A gentleman answered and invited her in. She was still nervous but decided that she would trust Ewan's visions. They were right every other time.

The rancher showed her to the kitchen and offered her a drink. "Hello, darlin'," he said to her. "What brings you all the way out here?"

Rylee had to look up at the rancher like she did with everyone else. He had sandy hair and warm eyes. His skin was tan from years of working in the sun. She took a deep breath before launching into the story. She explained the busload of kids that she and Ewan had rescued that needed somewhere safe to stay and the extreme danger they were in from Mr. B.G.

"My friend had a vision that we would be safe here," she told him, wrapping up her story. "Was he right?"

The rancher took her hand in both of his and looked

her in the eyes. "I knew this day would come, as I had a vision as well. Of course, your children will be safe here. I have plenty of space. Is anyone injured? I can have a nurse here in about ten minutes."

Rylee relaxed a bit at his words. She knew that she was dealing with someone else who had visions, so he wouldn't think that any of this was insane or out of the ordinary.

"Nobody seemed physically injured, but I don't know if they are malnourished or have any injuries that didn't heal correctly. My friend has told me some pretty brutal stories about what these kids have been through," Rylee told him, realizing she had no idea if anyone was nursing an injury that wasn't apparent on the surface. "Can I bring them into the house? I have teenagers watching a bunch of scared kids in a small space, and I feel like this isn't going to end well if we don't give them some relief." She smiled at the thought of the little ones getting rambunctious and the teens losing their minds.

"Of course, I can help lead them to the house. I will have one of my ranch hands move your bus to a more inconspicuous location so people driving down the road won't know anything is different," the rancher said as he led her back outside. "You can call me Hank, by the way. What is your name?"

"Rylee. Thank you, Hank," she said, feeling some relief.

They returned to the bus and helped the kids off of the bus. Once all of the kids were safely inside, Hank called his nurse to do some precautionary exams on some of the smaller kids; they looked underweight and a bit pale for his liking. His next call was on a secure line to the local police department. Mr. B.G. kidnapped most of these kids, and he wanted to make sure they could eventually be returned to their families. Others were street kids; they needed supportive foster homes set up so that they could learn to control their powers and live happy lives away from crime and death for as long as possible.

Once those details were sorted and the kids were entertained by life on the ranch, Rylee, Ewan, Hank, and a couple of the oldest teenagers sat down in the kitchen to discuss their next steps. While the ranch was safe for now, Mr. B.G. and his gang would find them soon.

"We are going to war, aren't we?" the young redhead finally asked.

"It certainly looks that way, Sami," another one responded.

"Hey, don't look so glum! We are going to figure this out," Rylee said with a sense of false bravado. "We are going to make this world safe for you again." She wasn't sure how she would make good on that, but she knew she was going to do it or die trying.

"Casey, I remember the day you came into the barracks," Ewan reminisced. "You were around nine years old and terrified. Do you remember?"

Casey thought for a moment, brushing his jet black hair out of his face before responding. "Yes, I remember. You gave me chocolate and let me sleep in your bed that night." He continued to recall. "You told me as long as you were alive; I had at least one friend here."

"That's right. Did I keep my promise?" Ewan asked.

"Yeah, I guess so." Casey stared at his feet. "But you got yourself killed! You left me!"

"I know, I'm sorry. But I am still here for you, even if I am not in the physical world. We are going to stand together." Ewan was on his feet in his physical form, but he didn't even notice. He just wanted these kids, his kids, to realize that he was there until the end.

Rylee sat back and watched Ewan work. He was

incredible. These teenagers, who the world had so hurt, really trusted him. They looked at him like he was their hero. She realized that he probably was; he probably saved each of their lives more than once as Mr. B.G. tried to break them. She loved watching him rally everyone together. He was also holding his physical form even though they hadn't touched since she went to find Hank. She wasn't sure what this meant, but she felt like this was probably a good sign. Maybe he would be able to pass back to the physical world when this was all over. But for now, they needed to focus on beating Mr. B.G. for good.

Once they had a general plan set up to defend the ranch and the kids who were too young to do much to protect themselves, they sent the teenagers to get showers and some rest. Ewan and Rylee made their rounds to check in on the younger kids. While Rylee worked with the kids, she found Ewan watching her with a soft look. His gaze started to draw her in, and she found herself constantly looking to see if he was still watching.

Rylee was amazed at how easily these city kids settled into country life. Some of them were helping in the barn, learning how to tend to the horses. Others were wandering through the vegetable gardens and crops under the ranch hands watchful eyes. Hank's wife had gotten the youngest of the bunch settled in for a nap. For now, their world was at peace. Rylee was happy that these kids were actually getting to be kids for once, even if that would be short-lived.

Hank pointed out the room that Rylee could use to rest, plan, and do whatever else she needed. Rylee was happy that she had somewhere to call her own again. Saturday morning seemed so long ago. She felt so lost since the break-in. The only time she felt anchored was when she was alone with Ewan. He felt like home. Maybe there was a way for them to be together after all. She needed to believe in something to get her through this fight, and right now, what she could believe in was the love she felt for Ewan.

Ewan settled into Rylee's bed while she washed her face and changed into something a bit more comfortable. Rylee watched him from the bathroom mirror. She could see him stealing glances, and she wanted him. She wasn't sure how that would work, if it would work, or if it was possible, but anything seemed possible these days.

"Ewan, I want to try something," Rylee began. She noticed that Ewan was spending more time in his physical form, and she wanted to see if they could be intimate together. "I have never heard of anyone being successful when trying to have sex with a spirit, but clearly, there is something more going on. Are you willing to try with me?"

Ewan was surprised by the request but eager to see what would happen. "Sure, just don't be disappointed if it doesn't work. Sex is not everything. I hope you know that sweetie," Ewan reassured her before she climbed onto the bed.

Since neither of them knew how this would work out, Ewan suggested that they start with him on top so Rylee didn't get hurt if something went awry. Ewan began by kissing her neck softly, eliciting a delighted gasp from Rylee's lips. He worked his way down her soft, tight body, kissing and nibbling every inch of skin he touched. Rylee was shocked as he gently slid inside of her after a few minutes of gentle foreplay. Somehow Ewan had found her most sensitive areas faster than any other guy she had dated before. Rylee knew at that moment that everything was going to be okay, she had no idea how, but it would be.

Ewan gently thrusts against Rylee's body. He increased his speed as Rylee's moans encouraged him. She wrapped her legs around his waist to pull him in closer. She had never had sex that felt this good before. Her hands wandered around Ewan's body, and she wondered if it felt good for him as well since he wasn't alive. She gently clawed his back as he continued to thrust and react to her moans and squeals of delight.

Rylee felt his motions slow and his hands still. She stole a glance and noticed the far-off stare that he got when he was having visions, but the pleasure of him was too great. Moments later, ecstasy exploded through her entire body, and she thrust her hips up to meet Ewan's. She had never felt anything so amazing in her life. She was left panting as Ewan rolled off of her; she needed a few minutes to catch her breath.

"Ewan, tell me about your vision," Rylee said once she could breathe again.

"I saw that we would be together long after all of this ends," Ewan told her with a smile.

"I know we will, baby, but I feel like there is more," Rylee urged him to continue.

Ewan paused. "It isn't completely clear, but I can see that I will have to make a big sacrifice to make that happen."

"Oh, Ewan! No, I don't want you to have to sacrifice to be with me; we should just be able to be happy together!" Rylee felt like crying. Why couldn't things just be straightforward after all of this chaos? "I will figure out a way that we can avoid that. I won't lose you, but I also won't let you lose anything to stay with me."

Ewan held her close and let her cry on his shoulder. "You need some sleep, come on, lay down," he urged, tucking her in. "I will be right here when you wake up."

ELEVEN

Things are Heating Up

RYLEE DRIFTED OFF TO SLEEP IN EWAN'S ARMS. SHE dreamt of a house with a yard, children running around, and Ewan holding her from the deck. It was everything she wanted. The sun warmed her face, a detail that could have been in the dream or in real life. Opening her eyes, she saw the sunlight through the window. Part of her mourned the end of the dream. Everything was so perfect.

She heard some of the kids laughing and playing outside of her window. Feeling the need to check on them, she found Ewan was still holding her.

"Can't I just stay here forever?" she asked, leaning her head into his chest.

Ewan floated around the room while Rylee got ready; he didn't feel a need to keep his physical form when he was alone. It seemed to be an unnecessary way to spend his energy. Once she was ready, they made their way out onto the ranch to see what everyone was doing.

The young girl from the bus the day before ran up to Rylee as soon as they stepped out of the house. "Horsey! Come look at the horsey!" she squealed in excitement.

Rylee let the small child take her hand and guide her to the paddock where the horses were grazing in the morning sun. "You are right. Those are horseys." Rylee crouched down to get on her level before asking, "What is your name, sweetie?"

"Mia! I'm Mia. You are pretty," Mia exclaimed.

There was something pure about how excitable and blunt little kids were when they had something on their minds. Rylee smiled and picked her up. "Thank you, Mia. How old are you, darling?"

Mia held up three chubby little fingers before squirming to get out of Rylee's arms. Once Rylee put her down, Mia ran off to find the teenager that held her on the bus to show her the horses.

"She's sweet." Rylee turned to Ewan to see if he knew more about the little tyke, but he was staring at something coming up the road.

Two detectives' cars pulled up to Hank's driveway. Rylee took a deep breath; it was common knowledge that one of the reasons the crime bosses were so effective was that they had dirty cops working for them. But once she closed the distance between herself and the cops that pulled up, she knew that these were not that kind of cops.

"Hello, detectives, what can we do for you?" Rylee asked.

"We came to see the children," the taller detective began. He had the look of someone who had been fighting the good fight for a long time. His brown hair was sprinkled with more than a little bit of gray. His hazel eyes were shrouded in dark and weathered circles. "Hank told us about your rescue mission. Great work getting so many children out of Mr. B.G.'s hands. We know that he is still out there, but we are searching for him. You will be safe soon, I promise."

"Thank you. My name is Rylee. I believe Hank is in the kitchen with his wife," Rylee said. "Follow me."

Rylee and the cops made their way into the main house to see Hank and his wife. "Detective Alvarado, it is so good to see you. I just wish it was under better circumstances!" Hank said as he hugged the detective.

"Do you think we could meet the children?" the shorter detective asked gently. She was clearly younger than Detective Alvarado. Her hair was tied back in a messy bun, and her eyes were still bright with the hope that they weren't fighting a losing battle. "We need to start figuring out who was kidnapped and who was taken off of the streets."

Ewan stepped forward and manifested into his physical form in front of their eyes. "These kids are in danger. We don't know who we can trust and who is in league with Mr. B.G. I watched too many cops either turn a blind eye or directly help him skirt the law. I will not let you start running these kids' names through your system. It will get them killed."

The detectives were stunned by his sudden appearance. Ewan wrapped his arm around Rylee and put his hand on the small of her back to show their connection. Once the detectives regained their senses, they were able to process his stern warning.

"We want to protect these kids, too," Detective Alvarado said in a measured tone. "How do you know all of this?"

"Mr. B.G. kidnapped me when I was eight and manip-ulated me into being one of his best cronies. I was trying to escape and help liberate these kids leading up to my own murder. I was the one who helped Rylee break into Mr. B.G.'s barracks and get these kids to safety. I am not about to let you risk it all to get a jump on some paperwork. I have worked too hard to throw it all away," Ewan explained.

"I should tell you. I am a medium. Everything he is telling you is the truth. We found his journals that document everything. Including his efforts to gain enough information to break free and help all of Mr. B.G.'s other recruits do the same. Mr. B.G. has a powerful hold on the kids he takes in. Somehow he can block their memories and control them. It has taken a lot for Ewan to be able to remember what happened to him. I agree. It is far too risky to let these kids' names start popping up in your databases. They are as safe as they can be here with us," Rylee told the detectives.

The detectives begrudgingly agreed. They informed them they would continue to search for Mr. B.G. before processing the lost children. Rylee, relieved that they had been convinced, led Ewan back to the bedroom. Her head was hurting. Spirits were everywhere. It felt like they were screaming at her to hear them.

"Rylee, I can feel them too," Ewan said, surprise in his tone. "Even the ones that are far away." His face fell as the realization donned on him. "Mr. B.G. has more kidnapped kids he's using to kill people... I knew and trained some of these kids..."

Through Ewan's concentration and focus, Rylee got a clearer image of one spirit. "Who is that?" she asked warily.

Ewan didn't respond immediately. He simply stared at the spirit that was calling to him. "That is Connor," he said in a choked, strained voice. "I would recognize his lankiness anywhere. He always kept his long curly hair in that weird half-bun thing, too. It has to be him."

"Connor, okay, why are you staring at him like that?"

Rylee tried to pull Connor in so they could communicate without the background noise.

"He might as well have been my brother... and now he is dead because of me." Ewan was pale, even for his spirit form. If Mr. B.G. wanted to hurt him, he certainly managed that.

"Ewan," Connor called, "I missed you, brother."

"What happened to you?"

"Once B.G. realized that you rescued most of his kids, he lost it. He sent everyone he still had under his control out to kill anyone who ever spoke against him. He held me back, though. I didn't understand why until he gave me a message for you as he slit my throat."

Rylee sent all of the other spirits away for a few moments to give Ewan and Connor some privacy. She could tell that this was important; Connor had the same look that Ewan did the first day she met him.

"Connor, what was the message?" she asked.

"Mr. B.G. wants you to know that you have two choices. You can either turn yourselves in, or he will kill Tarsizio," Connor said.

TWELVE

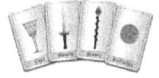

The Decision Is Made

RYLEE SANK INTO THE CHAIR IN THE CORNER OF THE ROOM. She knew that she couldn't turn Ewan over to Mr. B.G., but she also couldn't just let her uncle die. Uncle Tars had not been the best person and definitely hid things from Rylee, but she still loved him. She loved Ewan, too; she didn't want to lose him. Rylee held her head in her hands, fighting back the tears.

Ewan thanked Connor for the information and told him that Rylee might contact him over the next few days as they prepare to fight. Connor was more than willing to bring his killer down and help protect Rylee and Ewan in any way he could. He drifted away to give Rylee and Ewan some privacy.

Ewan made his way to Rylee. "Sweetie, I know this is a lot to take in. But I have seen this all in my visions. You are going to survive this, more than survive, you are going to thrive." Ewan coaxed her head out of her hands and looked her in the eye before gently kissing her forehead.

"But how? I can't choose between you and my uncle.

He is the only family I have left, and you know I can't live without you," Rylee said, distraught.

"I have seen many different versions of events for the coming fight. There are many variables that will determine how it turns out, but the one thing that never changes is that you are always safe in the end," Ewan reassured her. "I won't hide this from you, though. Your uncle does not survive every scenario. I will do my best to protect him, but you have to understand that you and the kids are my top priorities."

"This is all so messed up. I don't understand how any of this even began. I can't believe that my life was normal, or as normal as life gets for a medium, up until that Saturday." Rylee shook her head, trying to remember what day it was. "The break-in feels so long ago. I just want it all to be over. I want to go home."

"Rylee, my dear, I know. I let Mr. B.G. kill me that day, so I could get the message to you. I knew that I needed to do something to protect you. I could have fought back, but I knew that I would be of more help to you once I crossed over into the spirit world."

"You. Did. What?" Rylee snapped.

"Baby, please calm down. It will be okay."

Rylee was furious. How could Ewan be so stupid? Rylee thought. He could be alive right now! He didn't have to die. None of this makes any sense. Why couldn't he have delivered the message to me while he was alive? Then we could have fought Mr. B.G. together from the beginning before all of this.

Rylee took a deep breath before speaking again. "Ewan, please explain to me why you had to die. I don't understand."

"Dying was the only way to break free of Mr. B.G. He had complete control over my every moment. There was no way I could have gotten to you before the break-in otherwise. I knew he was going to kill me soon. He was starting to notice that I was asking too many questions. I was keeping to myself when I wasn't on jobs, and I was always writing," Ewan explained. "He couldn't afford to let me go and do my own thing, I knew too much, but he also realized that I was a danger to everything he worked so hard for over the past twenty-five years. He trusted me with too much information, and my visions allowed me access to things that nobody else knew, even the other Powered People."

Rylee gaped at him. How could Ewan be so cavalier about his own death? "Is there more?" she asked, readying herself for the entire story; she needed the information to be able to move forward in this fight.

"I put up a bit of a fight when he came to kill me. I didn't want to make him anymore suspicious of me. If he had known I wanted to die, he would have kept me alive by any means possible; that was just how he operated. I must have had that notebook about you in my bag when he killed me, which is how he and his goons had it at that pizza place. I should have known better; I hope you can forgive me for that oversight."

Rylee continued to stare, open-mouthed.

"I knew that you were the key to bringing Mr. B.G. down and that I had to get to you. I must have had new visions right before he summoned me; that part is still a little hazy. I didn't count on losing my memory when I died; that was a very inconvenient little trick B.G. pulled on me. But spending time with you, I have been able to get most of my memory back for some reason. I'm certainly not complaining about that fact..." Ewan trailed off.

Rylee threw her arms around his neck. "Ewan, I had no idea about any of this. I know that it has been a long and crazy time for you. Thank you for protecting me," Rylee said, bursting into tears.

"Why are you crying?"

Rylee sniffed and smiled meekly. "Sorry, I am just trying to process everything, and I'm so full of emotion right now. I know this will work out in the end because of all you have sacrificed. I hate the thought that you have had to, but I am so grateful that you did."

"I had to; it was not a choice. I knew that being with you was the only answer," Ewan stated simply.

Rylee released her ironclad embrace on his neck and looked him in the eye. "Ewan, you are a very special person."

Rylee gave him a soft kiss and left to dry her eyes and wash the tears off her face. When she returned, Ewan motioned for her to sit next to him on the bed.

"Rylee, there is more that you need to know," Ewan said carefully.

"You might as well just tell me everything right now. Who knows how much time we have left before this all blows up," Rylee responded.

"Alright, just listen to me before you respond, please," Ewan requested.

"Of course." Rylee pretended to zip her lips and throw away the key.

Ewan's serious expression split into a warm smile at the action. "I have seen more visions about you recently. You are bringing people back to life, but they aren't quite the same when you do. I can't really explain why that happens, but it does. These people you bring back also serve you. It's like they are bound to do your bidding or something. It all seems to be for the betterment of the cause, but it isn't clear how or why they are obeying you.

"I can see that we will need these souls to fight Mr.

B.G. and the army he will bring to fight us. This fight will not be easy. It will feel like an all-out war. I would love to say that the good guys all live and the bad guys all die, but that isn't how war works, unfortunately. But we can win this, Rylee."

She sat there quietly, absorbing everything Ewan was telling her. She had heard of people who could bring spirits back from the dead, but she never paid much attention to the stories. 'Reapers,' were they? Now she focused on the fact that they could win. That was all that mattered.

"How do we save my uncle?" she asked, afraid of what the answer might be.

"I don't know. There are many outcomes. Sometimes he survives, and sometimes he doesn't. If your priority is to save him, he dies, and Mr. B.G. gets away with all the kids. I'm sorry, Rylee."

Rylee was not entirely sure she understood, but there was no reason to shoot the messenger. "I can't focus on saving him," she said. "I know what I have to do."

"No matter what, I assure you, no harm will come to you. Your uncle is your only family. I am not asking you to give that up. You have time to think about this," Ewan told her. "It's a big decision."

"I am not going to kill him or sacrifice him, but as you said, that's not the main focus," Rylee said. "I can't risk Mr. B.G. winning just to keep one person alive, as much as I want to." She looked out the window at the children playing. "They're so innocent, and we're responsible for them now. I can't let him win."

There wasn't much more to say. Ewan hugged her tight before making their way into the kitchen to discuss what they knew with Hank. He deserved as much after all he had done for them.

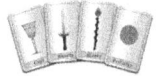

THIRTEEN

Missing Pieces

WITH HANK UP TO SPEED, RYLEE GATHERED ALL THE children in the barn. She would prefer they all stayed away from the fight, but she knew the teenagers and young adults among them should be allowed to choose. Some of them had been fighting for more than a decade against Mr. B.G.'s control to no avail. And many of them had powers that could be useful.

Once it was decided who among the teenagers and young adults would stay and fight, the crowd dispersed to train and prepare. Hank's wife would watch the younger children and keep them calm. She was already working to make sure they had food, water, and medical supplies. She adopted little Mia as her number one helper, mainly to keep her busy and away from the older kids who were actively preparing for an all-out war. Mia didn't need to see that.

Rylee talked with Sami and Casey and a few others when a car drove up to the ranch. Everyone was already on high alert. The teenagers who were training around them fell into a fight formation behind her. Nobody recognized the woman who stepped out of the car. She was easily as tall as Hank. She wore a tight pencil skirt and blazer. Her auburn hair was in a tight bun at the top of her head. She was clearly not someone to be trifled with. She wasn't one of Mr. B.G.'s known associates, but nobody knew how far his influence reached.

Casey stepped in front of Rylee to greet the woman and make it known that Rylee was protected. He was nearly a foot taller than Rylee and was highly muscular for his age.

"Who are you? Why are you here?" Casey asked bluntly; he didn't have time for small talk.

Ewan appeared next to Rylee for added emphasis. Rylee could sense his hesitation; he didn't recognize her either.

"I am here to see Rylee," she said, unfazed by either Ewan or Casey. "I am not associated with the man you are planning to fight. I need to speak to you and Ewan in private, please. I mean you no harm, but what I have to tell you is important in your coming battle."

"Stand down," Rylee told the kids, "go back to training. I will be okay." She admired their support, but something in her heart told her to trust this strange woman.

"Miss Rylee, with all due respect, I would feel better if one of us came with you," Casey said. He kept the newcomer in his line of sight at all times.

"I will be okay, but if you would feel better, you can wait right outside of my room while we talk. Does that work for you?" Rylee reasoned with him.

"That is fine," Casey responded.

"Alrighty then, let's let everyone else get back to what they were doing and go have a chat," Rylee said with confidence. The teenagers scattered as Rylee led Ewan, Casey, and the mystery woman back to the house.

When they arrived, Casey pulled Rylee aside as the others entered the room. "Be careful, Rylee. I've seen Mr. B.G.'s tactics firsthand."

Rylee gave him a hug. "I will be okay. You will be right here," she assured him. He was a sweet kid that had seen too many horrors at his age. She gave him a confident nod and joined the others.

"What do you want?" Rylee said once the door was firmly closed behind her. She had put on a friendly face in front of the kids, but she was not about to mince words now that it was just her, Ewan, and this woman. Even Ewan was caught off guard by Rylee's sharp tone.

"My name is Alicia. I was a friend of your parents," she began. "I had known them since before you were born. They are good people."

"You mean 'were' good people. They have been dead for five years," Rylee snapped at her.

"No, I said what I meant. Your parents are not dead," Alicia explained. "They are reapers, and the day of the car accident, they moved on to the next level of Reaperdom. I have information your parents wanted to share on your eighteenth birthday."

"What are you talking about?"

Alicia sighed with exasperation. "Your uncle was supposed to tell you this! Your family comes from a long line of Reapers. There are Living Reapers, like what your mother was before the accident and Dead Reapers. Dead Reapers are more powerful but, for all outward appearances, dead. Your uncle really didn't tell you?"

"No! No, he didn't." Rylee felt the anger rising as she spoke. "He didn't tell me any of this! He let me believe that my parents were dead. Why would he do this?!" Her voice started to rise before she remembered Casey on the other side of the door. She quickly composed herself as Alicia began to continue.

"He knew the family history better than anyone. Usually, after the death of one Reaper, another awakens. When your mother died, his powers didn't awaken, but yours did. Too young. We've been keeping an eye on him. He is jealous and resentful, and we think he may be involved.

"We have been watching you, Miss Rylee; you have done well as you learned about your powers. Not once have you tried to use them for power or crime. But you must know that your love for Ewan is going to change everything."

"Alicia, please talk to me like I'm five," Rylee said. "Uncle Tars never explained anything. He told me to keep my distance from my abilities. I just wanted to be a normal kid when my parents died, moved on, or whatever you called it. Now I just want to live a normal adult life. I want to help people. That is why I love the work I do at my family's store. Sometimes I felt trapped there, but I still loved it," Rylee said, trying not to get too frustrated with Alicia. It wasn't Alicia's fault that Tarsizio hid everything from her.

Ewan sat quietly on the bed while Rylee paced around the room, processing everything.

"I will explain everything your uncle should have years ago," Alicia said. "Please take a deep breath. You have latent reaping abilities, awakened when your parents ascended. This is why you can communicate with spirits. Usually, the previous generation has more time to tell their children and train them. Still, someone had other plans for your parents.

"Your father decided to pass over to the other side on

the day of the accident, and both of your parents became Dead Reapers. Your mother had no choice. They were joined from the day that she claimed his soul to unlock her reaping abilities. She was brought to the other side with him. She has been watching over you but could not communicate with you; it is against the rules. This is why most parents choose not to move on until they have had time to prepare their children for what will happen next.

"The accident wasn't your father's fault. His choice to become a Dead Reaper and dragging your mother with him on that day was, however. He hopes he can explain it to you one day. Your mother resents him for taking the choice away from her.

"If you become a Reaper and embrace your abilities, you will become one of the most powerful and youngest, Living Reapers that existed in the past 300 years. But it is a choice you have to make." Alicia hated to dump this all on the young lady, but Rylee needed to have all of the information possible. "Mr. B.G. is flooding the spirit world and causing turmoil between both realms."

"One of the most powerful reapers? Would I be strong enough to take down someone like Mr. B.G.? Will it keep these kids safe?" Rylee asked. This seemed to be the secret weapon she needed to defeat him, and she wasn't going to balk at the opportunity. She had a gut feeling that this was also the missing ingredient that would allow her and Ewan to be together for a long time.

"Yes. That doesn't mean it will be easy, but you will be able to do it," Alicia answered. She didn't want to influence Rylee in either direction. Still, she knew that embracing her abilities would be the best thing for both the physical and spirit worlds.

"I will do it. I need every tool available to bring him

down. I will not let him win," Rylee told her. "What do I have to do?"

"You can awaken your Living Reaper status by claiming Ewan's soul," Alicia said simply. "Before you face Mr. B.G., you probably want to claim a few souls of your own."

FOURTEEN

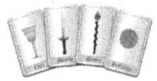

Becoming a Reaper

RYLEE STARED AFTER ALICIA, THEN AT EWAN. THIS WAS all moving too fast.

What does she mean by 'claim Ewan's soul?' That sounds...dangerous, she thought. *What could she mean by 'claiming a few souls of my own.'?*

Alicia stood to leave before Rylee could ask anything else. Rylee's head was still spinning. By the time she could form a question, Alicia had vanished.

"Ewan!" Rylee exclaimed. "What should I do?"

Ewan wrapped his arms around Rylee, hoping to calm her down. This was a lot of information to get after so many years. "Rest for now. I can't begin to imagine how overwhelmed you are," Ewan said, carrying her back to the bed.

"But there is so much to do!" Rylee began before Ewan raised his finger to her lips.

"Let me figure some things out. I need to know you are resting so I can focus. I promise I will wake you as soon as I know anything," Ewan reassured her before turning the light off and closing the door.

How am I supposed to rest when I just learned that my father decided to leave me behind with this mess? I could have had graduation pictures with my mother if it wasn't for him. Rylee's mind continued to race, but eventually, the mental and physical exhaustion won out, and she drifted off to a night of restless sleep.

///

"WHAT WAS THAT ABOUT?" Casey asked Ewan.

"Rylee just learned new information about her family that she should have known well before now. Leave her to rest, and you better not ask her about it," Ewan warned.

"Yes, Sir," Casey saluted before he returned to training with the others.

Ewan made his way to the living room where Hank was sitting with his newspaper. "Hank," he said quietly. "Is there somewhere I could go to be alone for a bit?"

"Of course." Hank guided Ewan to a room far away from where the children stayed and left him alone to think.

Ewan took a deep breath, a habit he got into when he was in his physical form even though he didn't actually need the oxygen. As he did, he began to get another vision. He closed his eyes to focus on what he was seeing. For a new Reaper to claim their first soul and activate their abilities, there had to be a deep emotional connection between the Reaper and the spirit. They needed to have as many points of contact as possible for this to work correctly. It seemed like a complicated process, but one they would do together. They had a chance to win this war. He was not going to waste it.

///

RYLEE FELT Ewan's soft kiss on her forehead. "I need you to wake up for me. I know what we have to do."

Rylee stretched and yawned as she woke. "You did it? You figured it out?" Rylee was still half asleep until she felt the excitement radiating off of Ewan's spirit, and that woke her right up. "Tell me what we have to do!"

Ewan sat on the bed with Rylee and pulled her into his arms. "Rylee, this is not going to be easy, but remember what we are fighting for. You are my soul mate; this will just make our bond permanent. Are you ready?"

"Ewan! Yes, tell me," Rylee was losing patience. She loved Ewan with all of her heart and needed to make sure that they were bonded before this fight. She shifted out of Ewan's arms and onto his lap.

"Alright, this is perfect. Now wrap your legs around my waist and your arms around my neck," Ewan explains. "The closer they are, the better. Now, you need to say the Reaper's Spell, do you know it?"

Rylee had to think about all of the spells she knew, racking her brain for the right one. It took some time, but she found it in the recesses of her mind. She closed her eyes and rested her forehead against Ewan's before reciting the spell. She finished and kissed Ewan. She felt his soul enter her body and bond with hers. She knew it worked, she claimed his soul, and they were eternally bonded; when Ewan dies or has met his redemption, they will move on and meet their parents in the next level of Reaperdom. Rylee melted into Ewan's arms. He was hers forever.

Ewan's body felt more and more solid with no energy drain from Rylee. He squeezed Rylee tightly in his arms. "Rylee! You did it, baby girl!" He kissed her again and let her slip off of his lap.

"Do you feel any different?" Rylee had no idea what

this would do to Ewan. She realized that she rushed ahead into this without even thinking. "Are you okay?"

"I feel fine! Alive!" He took a real breath this time. "I saw this happening; everything went exactly the way it was supposed to," Ewan said confidently. "There is one big difference. But I knew that was coming."

Rylee raised an eyebrow. "What is that?"

"Remember that I did this voluntarily," Ewan began, "I don't have my visions anymore."

Rylee was ready to lose her mind. "You what?!"

"When I was trying to understand the process earlier, I saw that I would lose my visions if you claimed my soul. I decided that staying with you forever and helping you unlock your reaping abilities was worth it." He didn't want her to be upset, but there was no point in lying to her. "I knew what I was doing, and I knew what would happen."

Rylee hated that Ewan had to make such a huge sacrifice for her to unlock her abilities. She felt selfish. "Are you sure it's okay?"

"Yes, Rylee, I am sure." Ewan kissed her again before getting up to shower.

Rylee decided once Ewan was done, she would take one of her own. Perhaps the hot water would do her some good.

"I haven't felt warm water since before I died," Ewan said when he returned. He spotted Rylee approaching the shower. "There should still be hot water left!"

Rylee felt more relaxed under the hot water instantly. She used the body wash, shampoo, and conditioner that were left in the shower. She hadn't thought about how long it had been since she washed her hair properly; it had grown a noticeable amount since then.

She dried off and noticed a change of clothes on the vanity that wasn't there before; Ewan must have left them for her. Rylee got dressed and braided her hair back before wrapping it into a bun. Long hair was great, but it tended to get in the way. She took one last look in the mirror before rejoining Ewan in the bedroom.

/ / /

A COUPLE WEEKS PASSED. The children's resolve strengthened, and Rylee's powers grew exponentially. She quickly learned how to not only reach out to spirits but to pull them into her grip and even under her will. She wasn't too fond of it, but sometimes unruly spirits needed the encouragement. Plus, it meant she would be able to turn spirits that died in the future battle on her side.

"Are you ready?" Ewan asked.

The day of the confrontation was upon them. Their army was ready. Most of them were already well-trained, thanks to their time at Mr. B.G.'s barracks. After their time at the ranch, they only grew stronger. Plus, Rylee had pulled many willing and eager souls onto their side from the afterlife.

"Let's do this," she said before she took his hand in hers.

Together, they gathered the older kids that insisted on joining them in this fight. They hugged Hank and his wife and promised that they would be back soon. Mia ran up to Rylee and attached herself to her leg. "Miss Rylee, take me with you," she cried.

"Mia, sweetie, I have a very important job for you while we are gone. Do you think you can handle it?" Rylee asked, thinking quickly.

"Yes! Yes, Miss Rylee," Mia said, already distracted.

"I need you to keep all your friends safe. Mr. Hank and

his wife can help you too. Can you do that?" Rylee asked Mia.

"I can do that! I will keep everyone safe," Mia jumped into action.

"I can't wait to hear your report when we return." Rylee picked her up and hugged her tight. "We will see you all soon."

While Rylee was reassuring the younger kids that they would see each other soon, Ewan was rallying the older kids on the bus. Rylee found him just as he finished his speech to them.

"Remember, you might see your friends and classmates fighting beside Mr. B.G. They are under his control, and we cannot show any weakness. Once Mr. B.G. is taken out, they should be released from his control, and we can try to bring them with us and help them find a better path. But for now, my main focus will be keeping all of you safe and bringing down Mr. B.G."

The kids were ready to fight. They had been through hell under Mr. B.G.'s control, and this was their chance to do something about it. By the time Rylee boarded the bus, the teenagers had talked to each other, and she could feel the energy radiating through the bus.

Rylee sat quietly while Ewan drove to Mr. B.G.'s compound. She was focused on collecting any spirits she came across to help them in their battle. Many of the spirits had either been killed by Mr. B.G. and his gang or knew of his crimes and wanted to help bring him down anyway. Rylee was still learning about her reaping powers but claiming souls came naturally for her.

Once they were within the city limits again, Rylee started making some calls. Thanks to Ewan's notes, they knew who might be willing to betray Mr. B.G. under the right circumstances. Since Ewan and Mr. B.G. were the only ones who actually knew most of the dirt on these guys, it was easy to promise them that they would no longer be blackmailed if they helped. Fighting Mr. B.G. was their way of gaining a bit of redemption.

It didn't take long for Rylee and Ewan to assemble an army. They had skilled fighters, the kids that Mr. B.G. trained for years, and the spirits that Rylee claimed for herself. They felt like they had a chance now. Rylee encouraged everyone to meet them a few blocks from the complex so they could approach as a united front and show Mr. B.G. that he was not going to win.

FIFTEEN

The Battle Begins

RYLEE'S SMALL ARMY STOOD IN FRONT OF MR. B.G.'S complex. Looking back at them, she wasn't afraid anymore. She had taken to her Reaper powers naturally and formed an amazing team behind her. Every one of them wanted Mr. B.G. dead. They had passion, something Mr. B.G.'s army would never have.

Mr. B.G. strode outside, dragging Tarsizio behind him. Her uncle found her in the crowd, his eyes pleading through his binds and gag.

"Rylee, it is so great to see you. I am happy to be able to facilitate this little family reunion," Mr. B.G. said; every word was dripping with disdain. He then removed Tarsizio's gag. "Say hello to your niece, Tarsizio. I want to hear you beg for your life."

"Rylee! Please, he promised me that he wouldn't hurt you if you just turned yourself over to him," Tarsizio begged.

"Uncle Tars," Rylee began, "I know everything you tried to keep from me. I will not back down."

"Everything?" Tarsizio rounded on his captor. "Mr.

B.G., back down. This is not going to end the way you expect. There is so much you don't know."

"Shut up, old man," Mr. B.G. said. He shoved the gag back into Tarsizio's mouth and pushed him to the side. "I see you have some friends. It was so nice of you to bring them to their deaths." Mr. B.G. was confident that this wouldn't last long.

"It is good to know that in eighteen years, you haven't changed, B.G.," Ewan said, stepping from behind the group of teens he was holding back from attacking before they were ready.

"Ewan, you are here. This is wonderful. Now I can kill your little girlfriend and still be able to communicate with you. She is just dead weight; one more body to keep alive." Mr. B.G. didn't bother to hide the glee in his voice. "If you apologize and return to my side along with all of my children, I promise to make her death quick." With a snap of his fingers, his own army falls into formation behind him.

"We can do that too," Ewan said as the city councilmen lined up behind Mr. B.G.

Ewan snapped his fingers, and the kids fell into their own formation. Rylee whistled, and the people who had come together for redemption fell in as well. She commanded her army of spirits in front of everyone else as the first line of defense. Rylee stood on the sidelines; her abilities would be better used if she were not actively engaged in the fight. She needed to be able to claim the fallen souls.

The fight began in an instant. The spirits helped to deflect a lot of the incoming fire. Once the battle got real, they paired off with each of the living soldiers to help them in their one on one fight where they could.

It was already proving to be a bloody war. Rylee felt an influx of spirits as the soldiers fighting with Mr. B.G.

succumbed to her army one by one. A few of the men who had returned for their redemption also lost their lives. The children were doing alright against the terrible system that enslaved them for years.

Bodies were falling everywhere, and it was hard to keep track of where the attacks were coming from. Luckily, Rylee's understanding of her powers has dramatically improved. She could direct the spirits that she had claimed to help block any friendly fire that might come across. She didn't want any of the kids accidentally killing their friends and having to live with that on top of everything else they had been through.

Casey directed his power at Mr. B.G.'s heart, but he managed to sidestep just enough to avoid them; Tarsizio was not so lucky. He took a direct hit from Casey's blast and crumpled instantly.

Rylee felt her stomach drop. She had only blocked friendly fire, not realizing her uncle was in the line of fire. She pulled his spirit under her control as his body died. She decided to keep his spirit in limbo for right now. She needed to focus on the fight at hand and not deal with family drama. She refocused to continue claiming the souls that fell around her.

It broke her heart to see so many die for this cause, but she knew there was no alternative. Either they stood and fought, or they surrendered and died anyway. At least now, she could allow them a chance at redemption. Mr. B.G. was not one for mercy, despite what he might have told her uncle. He was ruthless.

///

EWAN AND SAMI were working together to bring down as many people at once. They didn't want this to continue any longer than it needed to; they both felt the need to protect the younger teenagers from bearing the brunt of the battle. But those kids were feisty; they were beating these seasoned fighters easily. They had clearly taken their training seriously over the past month at the ranch and didn't want to miss a moment of action.

In the crowd, Ewan found Mr. B.G. in a corner. With several well-placed blows, Ewan brought him to his knees.

"I bet you regret teaching me all about pressure points, don't you?" Ewan asked, standing over the man.

Mr. B.G. spat in his face.

"Well, if that is how it is going to be, we can end this now. There is no redemption for you. Every day of your adult life, you had a choice, and you chose violence. You chose to destroy people's lives, children's lives. There is no coming back from that. I hope you have made peace with your maker," Ewan said.

"You can go to hell, Ewan. I gave you everything, and this is how you repay me?"

"Enough," Ewan spat. He took a deep breath and quickly twisted Mr. B.G.'s head in his hands, severing his spine and killing him instantly.

Ewan sank down against the wall and held his head in his hands. He finally did it. He ended Mr. B.G.'s reign of terror. The powered kids would not have to worry about being taken from their families and corrupted. But taking a life made him feel sick, and his stomach lurched.

RYLEE FOUND Ewan next to Mr. B.G.'s body. She felt the relief and pain radiating through his soul. She stopped claiming souls to focus on her true love.

"Ewan, you did it. You ended everything. The kids are

free, and the people who stood with Mr. B.G. have scattered." Rylee kissed his forehead and hugged him for what seemed like forever.

"Rylee," Ewan said in a small voice, "he raised me. He was the only father figure I remember, and I killed him with my bare hands."

Rylee felt the emotions that were playing across his face deep within her soul. "Oh, Ewan, you know you had no other choice. I can't even begin to imagine how hard this is for you. But we will get through this together. I promise."

Ewan was quiet for a while before he managed to get his voice to work again. "Mia is safe," he finally blurted out. "That's what this fight was about. It was about little Mia and all the kids who still had a chance at a normal life." Ewan was starting to recenter himself; he allowed Rylee to help him to his feet.

The love Rylee felt for Ewan only seemed to increase the farther they got from the end of the fight. She could think about something other than surviving the next ten minutes. She allowed herself to think about having an amazing life together.

"Think about what these kids learned today. They saw good triumph, and they saw people making hard decisions. Those lessons can't be taught anywhere else."

"They will know they have a choice, even if all seems lost," Ewan said. "I hope they will always make the choice to do good." He picked up Rylee and kissed her forehead.

Rylee wrapped her legs around Ewan's waist; she had no intention of letting him put her down any time soon. She hadn't noticed how much taller than her he was until this instant, but she didn't care. He was hers, now and forever. Everything else would have to fall in around them one way or another.

Sami found Ewan and Rylee after she had rounded up

all of the kids that had been under Mr. B.G.'s powers until the end. "Oh, uhh, am I interrupting something?" Sami stuttered, blushing and averting her gaze.

Rylee giggled and squirmed out of Ewan's arms before straightening her outfit. "Not at all, dear," Rylee said. "Is everything okay?"

"Oh, yeah. I have the kids getting checked out to make sure nobody is badly injured. I think they mostly have a few cuts and scrapes," Sami told her. She was staring at her feet and refused to look Rylee or Ewan in the eye.

"Sami, what aren't you telling us?" Ewan asked, getting concerned.

"Ewan, I…" she started before bursting into tears.

"Oh, Sami, you can tell me, you know everything will be okay," Ewan hugged her in an attempt to calm her down.

"Ewan, did you know I have a kid?" Sami sniffed.

"I didn't, Sami. How old are they?"

"Three. You already met her, and she adores you and Rylee," Sami said as she regained control over herself.

Rylee realized who she meant. That was why Mia was there, she was too young to be of any use to Mr. B.G., but Sami didn't have anyone else to take care of her. "Sami! Mia is precious. You have done an amazing job with her, especially given the circumstances," Rylee hugged her and Ewan. "Now you can have a normal life with your daughter."

"Nobody else knows that she is mine. I don't know if I am ready for them to know," Sami told them. "Connor and I fell in love while we were cooped up in that awful place. Our hormones were raging like typical sixteen-year-olds, and we got a little bit carried away one night. Now he is dead, and I have to raise her alone. Our lives won't be normal. I have never had a normal life." Sami barely stopped herself from crying again.

"We won't tell anyone, promise. You can make a normal life for Mia," Ewan said. "Now, let's get back to the group so we can head back to your baby." Ewan wrapped his arm around her shoulder in support.

SIXTEEN

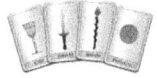

Life After Mr. B.G

SAMI, EWAN, AND RYLEE REJOINED THE GROUP AND HELPED get everyone loaded back onto the bus. There was a sense of relief in the air mixed with sadness. These kids knew nothing but Mr. B.G.'s control for so many years. A few were excited, but most of them were tentative and unsure of what the future would hold. They knew that they had done terrible things while under B.G.'s control and didn't know if they would be punished for it.

Sami checked in on everyone as they made their way back to the ranch. She was a caregiver. That was why nobody batted an eye at how she cared for little Mia. It was natural for her, and nobody bothered to question where the infant came from all those years ago because Mr. B.G. didn't have morals. He would rip a newborn from her mother's teat if he had an inkling that her powers would help him down the road.

Ewan pulled up to the ranch and saw that the detectives were back. Before he let the kids off the bus, he explained that the only reason the detectives were there was to help find their families. He reassured them that

111

nobody would be held accountable for the crimes that Mr. B.G. made them commit. He fielded a couple of questions from those who had not been able to escape with them initially. Then, once everyone seemed satisfied, he let them off the bus.

Hank and his wife were waiting on the porch to receive everyone. They hugged and kissed the children that returned and shook the hands of the newcomers. Mia was the first one to greet everyone once they entered the house. They felt the collective sigh of relief once those that had been left behind realized that all of their friends were back. Ewan and Rylee brought up the rear and closed the door behind them.

"Rylee! I kept everyone safe, just like you said!" Mia squealed as she launched herself into Rylee's waiting arms.

"I knew I could trust you, Mia. Great job!" Rylee squeezed her before setting her down. Mia ran to Sami and climbed into her lap.

"We are safe now. There is nothing to fear," Ewan began, and all eyes snapped to him. "The detectives need information from all of you. Please tell them anything you know. Our first priority will be to help you find your parents or families, but do not worry. If we can't, we will make sure you are all well taken care of and given the support you need to process everything we have experienced. Rylee and I will stay in contact no matter what. I am deeply sorry that it took this long for us to bring Mr. B.G. and his gang down."

The children all started applauding Ewan as he finished speaking. It caught him off guard. Casey hugged him, followed by Sami, who still had Mia in her arms. Little Mia kissed Ewan on the cheek.

"Thank you all for fighting beside us," Ewan concluded. "Rylee and I need a few moments to tie up loose ends. Please try to relax, and remember, tell the detectives whatever you can remember." He guided Rylee back to her room so they could get some privacy.

"Ewan, what do I do about Uncle Tarsizio?" Rylee asked. "I don't know if I should allow him a chance at redemption or if I need to send him on to face the consequences of his actions. He could have stopped this all!" She sank onto the bed. The pressure was already intense, and there was a sense of grief and loss tugging at her heart. He was the only family she had for the last five years. Even if he could have stopped it, even if she resented him for his actions, part of her still felt that loss.

"Sweetie, I can't make that decision for you. Remember, we all have choices to make; he decided to be jealous and devious. Whatever you decide, do it for yourself. You owe him nothing," Ewan reasoned, wrapping his arm around her shoulders.

Rylee sighed. This was probably one of the most challenging choices she had to make. Why did he have to choose jealousy? Why couldn't he just accept that he didn't have to take on the responsibility that the reaping abilities gave my mom? Why did he have to work against me? These questions kept running in circles around her brain. She knew what she had to do, but doing it was a whole different story.

"I can't save him, Ewan. As much as I may want to allow him a chance at redemption, I can't do it." Rylee rested her head on Ewan's chest before she got up to connect with the spirit world.

Her uncle was in limbo, and it was time. He had to face the consequences of his actions. Her parents were on the other side to greet him and do what needed to be done. A single tear escaped her eye as she realized that she had no family in the physical world. She had Ewan, which was more than she could have ever hoped for, but saying goodbye to her uncle was still gut-wrenching.

/ / /

A FEW DAYS passed at the ranch while the detectives were sorting through their missing child records from the past twenty years. It was amazing how many cases could now be closed. A few children were taken off of the street, and no reports were ever filed. Sami was one of those children; she lived on the streets fifteen years ago, and nobody ever filed a missing person report. Ewan asked Rylee if she would mind taking Sami back to the occult shop with them to help her get on her feet since she didn't have a family to return to and had a child to take care of. Rylee was eager to agree.

The four of them said goodbye to Hank and his wife, promising to keep in touch. The drive back to the shop was quiet, except for Mia happily pointing out every cow, horse, and goat she saw. Every now and then, there was another animal to excite her, like a pigeon or crow.

Rylee was lost in thought while Ewan drove them back to the shop. What am I going to do with this shop? I know I can do more than this with my life. I am meant to help people. How can I do that if I am tied down here? Rylee thought as they pulled up to the shop. It looked exactly as it had the day she ran for her life, but it felt very different. She got out of the car and walked up to the front of the shop, staring at the broken windows. I owe it to my family to keep it running. I owe Ava her job. Maybe I can do both; save people and run this shop.

Ewan and Sami came up on either side of her and wrapped their arms around her. They wanted to know that she was not in this alone. She rested her head on Ewan and wrapped her arm around Sami's waist. At that moment, she realized that she did have a family, the three people standing beside her. She led them inside to begin the clean-up after showing Sami a safe place where Mia could play.

Once they cleaned up the broken glass and scheduled someone to come and replace the glass, they sat down to discuss what was next for all of them. "The shop will be busy once we reopen, we are the best in town, and I know our customers will have missed us," Rylee explained. "Sami, how would you like to run the store for me?"

"Me? Run the store? I-I have no experience!"

"You will be fine! I saw how you were with the kids back at the ranch and after the fight. You truly care about people, and that is the most important thing here," Rylee told her, clutching her hand. "I can teach you the rest, but I can't teach people how to care. I have run the shop for my uncle since my parents passed away, or well, moved on, never mind, it isn't important. What matters is that this shop has been in my family for generations, and I want to keep it in the family."

Sami blushed as Rylee's words sunk in. "Oh, Rylee!" Sami threw her arms around Rylee's neck. "Of course I will."

///

EWAN SAT BACK, watching the girls plan out how the shop would be run and what they wanted to change. They were fascinating. If Ewan were not connected to Mia so intimately, he wouldn't be able to follow anything that they were saying.

They chatted for hours about work, so Ewan wandered off to play with Mia. He took her to the corner store to get lunch for everyone. He let Mia pick out a snack; as long as she promised not to tell her mommy. He enjoyed how her eyes lit up at the opportunity for a secret treat.

By the time he returned with their food, Sami and Rylee had sorted out most of the shop's details. Rylee had even offered Sami the apartment upstairs that had belonged to Tars before he died. It was owned by the shop so that it would be rent-free. They could clean it out and set up a bedroom for each of the girls and even a playroom for Mia. Sami decided that she was just going to accept it and not question Rylee. It was apparent that this was what made her happy.

/ / /

EWAN HELPED them rearrange some of the heavy furniture before they brought Mia upstairs. It still needed some work, but it was Sami's.

"Sami, tomorrow we will plan for a reopening date and a party of sorts, but for tonight, enjoy your space. Order something delicious for dinner, and call me if you need anything at all," Rylee gave Sami twenty dollars for dinner. "Good night, Mia, give me kisses!"

Mia didn't need telling twice; she jumped into Rylee's arms and gave her a big, wet kiss. "Rylee, is this really where I live now?" Mia asked.

"Yes, it is, princess," Rylee responded, smiling, "this is where you and your mommy live. Safe and sound."

Mia wiggled out of her hands and ran around the apartment. "You are definitely going to have your hands full with that one," Ewan chuckled. "Good night, Sami."

Ewan and Rylee made their way back to Ewan's apartment; it felt like the logical place to go. When they arrived, they realized that the apartment had been cleaned and the door had been replaced. They looked at each other and smiled. "Mr. Kildare," they said in unison. They would have to figure out how to repay him one day. But tonight, they just enjoyed each other's company.

They were relaxing on the couch together when Rylee sat up suddenly. "We are going to have a family together, aren't we?"

Ewan smiled from ear to ear. He pulled Rylee closer. "I want to tell you the last vision I had. I was grilling in the yard in summer. You were playing with three children— our three children—in the pool. We were all happy and safe." He gave her a long kiss. "I promise I won't do what your dad did. I won't redeem myself fully until our kids are ready to be Reapers themselves."

///

TOGETHER EWAN, Rylee, and Sami ran A Daily Dose of Crystal. Rylee did not feel tied to the shop anymore since Sami and Ava had it under control. She was free to help souls in need of redemption and those that simply needed a helping hand to get to the other side.

She had many discussions with Ewan about starting their own family and giving their children everything that they missed out on in life. Rylee was satisfied that Ewan understood the gravity of his choices. Rylee was ready to start a family immediately. She stopped her birth control the very next day.

Shortly before Mia's fourth birthday, Rylee and Ewan invited Sami, Mia, and Ava to dinner. They had important news to share. Rylee was expecting twins. Sami and Ava squealed in excitement while Mia just stared at her.

Rylee realized that Mia had no idea why her mom and Ava were squealing like that. "Babies are growing in my belly, Mia," Rylee explained. "Soon, it will get really big, and then before you know it, you will have two little cousins to play with and love."

Mia's eyes grew to the size of saucers, and she looked at Sami. "Rylee has babies in her tummy!"

"Yes, she does, sweetheart," Sami responded.

"I want to touch them!" Mia squealed.

Sami and Rylee laughed. "You can touch my tummy, but you won't feel them yet." Rylee took Mia's hand in hers, placed it on her stomach, and then moved it to Mia's. "See, my belly feels just like yours, but we are going to watch it grow, and then I will let you touch it as much as you want. Does that sound okay?"

Mia nodded. "Yes! Yes!" she squealed.

Rylee picked her up and looked around the room. She was so grateful for her little family. It had been a long and trying year for all of them, but they all stuck together and made it through. She looked forward to one day in the future becoming a Dead Reaper and reuniting with her parents. Still, she wanted to live a long and happy life in the physical world first. She had a responsibility to all of the people in this room. Ewan was standing by her side the whole time. He was her anchor. She felt Ewan wrap his arms around her and Mia before he kissed her gently on the forehead.

About the Author

Renee Joiner has been in love with the supernatural for longer than she can remember, so it is no surprise that she is an author of paranormal urban fantasy. Although she discovered her passion for writing when she was only twelve years old, she didn't make her writing debut until many years into the future. Adventurous and fun-loving, she enjoys traveling to new places, exploring new sights and meeting new people. Thus, she delights in creating fantastical worlds that are sure to give her readers an escape from the real world while simultaneously providing thrilling entertainment.

Besides her special knack for writing, you'll also find a passion for metaphysics spirituality which she has been nurturing for over four decades. Renee hails from New York and currently resides with her husband in their empty nest—unless you count their three adorable fur babies—in Florida. She enjoys adding to her sea of knowledge and thus spends her free time learning new things.

To find out more about Renee Joiner, feel free to visit her **official website**.

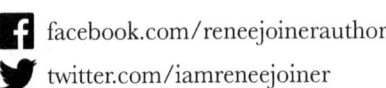

facebook.com/reneejoinerauthor

twitter.com/iamreneejoiner

instagram.com/reneejoinerauthor

amazon.com/author/reneejoiner

Series by Renee

Thorne Sisters Chronicles
Possessed by Magic
Reincarnated by Magic
Immortal by Magic

SIGN UP TO RECEIVE MY NEWLETTER FOR ALL THE LATEST UPDATES AND SPECIALS!

RENEEJOINERAUTHOR.COM/NEWSLETTER

Thank You..

Thank you for reading my book!
I really appreciate all of your feedback and I love to hear what you have to say. Please leave your review at your favorite retailer!